Casey

Casey

by Robert Spraker

Walker and Company
New York

First published in the United States of America
in 1984 by the Walker Publishing Company, Inc.

Published simultaneously in Canada by John Wiley & Sons
Canada, Limited, Rexdale, Ontario.

ISBN: 0-8027-4035-9

Library of Congress Catalog Card Number: 83-040418

Printed in the United States of America

10 9 8 7 6 5 4 3 2 1

CHAPTER 1

CASEY lay beside William and listened to the night sounds.

They're not as scary now as they were at first, she thought. Maybe in six months the sounds won't frighten me at all.

She lay and listened to the sound of the coyote in the distance and then snuggled a little closer to her husband. Casey ran an exploratory hand down his chest. She felt the familiar thrill as her hand hesitated for a moment on the hardness of his stomach. Then she let her hand slide slowly downward and come to rest. She left her hand there and waited to see if there would be a response.

There was nothing except a slight stirring of the man's body as Tige started his barking in the distance.

Tige's after a rabbit, she thought, and began to move her hand slowly. When nothing happened, she put both hands behind her head and listened to Tige chase the rabbit.

I love it! I love it. I love it all, she thought, and let her mind drift back to the whirlwind that hit her when she first met William Lee—how he saw through her as though she had been made of glass and how he refused to respond to all the special things she had learned from the other girls at Miss Brimley's school.

Casey smiled into the darkness as she remembered the look on Miss Brimley's face when she told the woman she was leaving school and how Miss Brimley had nearly lost the poise she taught her students so well.

"You're leaving Boston? And going where? With someone named William Lee? No proper wedding or anything? I simply will not believe you would do such a thing, my dear."

Even now Casey could feel the anger that had filled Miss Brimley's office as the older woman's voice rose to a screech.

Casey had sat on the edge of her chair and tried not to grip the roll of paper in her hand so hard it would crush.

"I had a proper wedding," she had said. "Judge Milton Brown said he was pleased to do it in his office and I have the license right here."

Casey had stared back at the woman then and said nothing more until Miss Brimley's face had softened and she had risen, come around her desk, and extended her hand.

"I really do wish you well, my dear. It's just such a . . . such a shocking thing for a Brimley girl to do. I'm sure your parents are furious."

When the woman's voice trailed off to nothing, Casey had simply nodded and left the room.

Casey turned on her side, put her arm around William, and drew herself closer to him. He's so strong, she thought, and he stood up to Father so well.

Casey closed her eyes and relived the hour she and Mother had spent listening outside the door of Father's study as William had tried to explain Texas to the older man.

She smiled as she remembered how Father had roared and how clearly the sound had come through the door. "Forget this foolishness! Stay in Boston. We will make arrangements at the bank. You could come in with me there or . . ."

Casey smiled again and pulled herself even closer to William as she recaptured the feeling of pride that had come to her when the time had come for William to roar at Father: "She is my wife, sir! And I will have her with me in Texas!"

Tige's bark was closer now and Casey wondered why the dog had not caught the rabbit yet.

He'll get him though. I'll bet he does.

Then she thought about the moonlit night that had started her on her long trek to Texas—how William's face had looked that night as the shadows of the leaves played upon it, so serious and grave as he talked to her about Texas and all that he hoped to do there, how he stammered a little when he proposed.

Tige sure is working that rabbit. Sounds like he's almost in the yard, Casey thought.

She put her hand back on William and started the slow movement again. Casey felt the response begin and then a sudden shock of hurt and anger as William rolled from the bed and strode to the window.

"William, I . . ."

"Shush!"

Casey joined him at the window and peered into the yard.

"There's somebody out there," he whispered.

"I don't see anyone, William. Who could it be?"

"I don't know, but they are there."

She sensed the strength of her husband's body as he crossed the room and took the Winchester from its place on the wall.

"Stay here," he said. "I'm going out. Lock the door behind me."

Casey followed him through the dark and waited for William to open the door. She heard him lift the heavy bar and the familiar squeak of the hinges. Then it seemed that everything happened at once.

She heard the heavy sound of the .44 and dampness hit her face as William's body slammed backward into her.

Casey lay on the floor and waited. She knew William was dead. She didn't have to think about it. She simply knew he was dead. She pushed with her feet and moved away from his body. The floor was rough against her bottom and she felt the cotton gown tear as she moved herself away from the horror and toward the little space between the wall and the wood box. She pushed again with her feet and hoped that she wouldn't make a sound.

She lay in the little space and bit the back of her hand to keep from screaming at the sound of boots scraping on the porch and the smell of a cigar. Casey wished she could faint but she could only watch and shake as the man's silhouette filled the doorway. Then she heard the sound of voices behind the man.

"I hope they's a woman. I need a woman bad."

Casey pulled her feet up under her and covered them with the gown. She bit her hand harder, held her breath, and stared into the darkness toward the door.

The salty taste of her blood in her mouth surprised her and she wondered why she would notice such a thing now.

She crouched and watched the outline of the man in the doorway as he fished in his pockets. Dimly, in the background, as though it were at a great distance, she heard Tige's snarls, and then, the sound of a shot. She waited and hoped to hear Tige again but there was only silence. Casey knew she was alone. The man in the doorway found the match and struck it on his belt buckle.

The sudden light blinded Casey but she knew the man was stepping over William's body and moving toward the lamp on the table. She tried to make herself as small as possible as the stranger lit the lamp.

She strained to control her shaking as the man called through the door into the darkness.

"Come get this mess out of here."

Casey watched the man move around the room in the lamplight as he took a pan of cold biscuits and meat from the safe and put them on the table and began to eat.

She listened to the ugly sloughing sound as the others dragged William's body to the porch and threw it into the yard. Casey bit into her hand again to hold back the scream and make it die in her throat.

Then the words hit her like a blow across the face.

"Damn. Ain't they no woman?"

"Yep."

"Where?"

"Over there behind the wood box shivering like a dog in a cold rain."

Casey heard the sound of a woman's voice screaming in the distance as everything around her went black.

***

Casey looked into the face of the man on top of her and opened her mouth to scream.

"Jist lie quiet, little lady, and I won't hurt you. I ain't the first. We let young Willie go first. He needed it bad."

She fought him then with every ounce of strength in her body. She fought and clawed and screamed. Once she felt her thumb in his eye and she tried to dig the eye out of his head. Then came the shock of his fist on her temple and she welcomed the darkness again.

***

Casey felt the warm tip of the spoon touch her lips. She took a little of the broth into her mouth, then let it trickle down her throat. She lay with her eyes closed and let the comfort of her mother's presence flow through her, waiting for the smell of lavender.

"Mama, Mama, I hurt so!"

She lay quietly and waited for her mother's soothing voice. When there was no sound, she opened her eyes and stared into the cold blue eyes of a man holding a spoon in one hand and a bowl in the other.

CHAPTER 2

CASEY closed her eyes quickly and tried to sink into the darkness again. The pounding in her head caused a constant ache, and she wondered if her heart could stay in her body while beating this way.

The spoon touched her lips again. She turned her head away without thinking, and squeezed her eyes shut as tightly as she could get them. She heard the short "Humph!" and then the movement of the man as he left her side.

Casey opened one eye and looked across the room at the stranger's back as he placed the bowl and spoon on the table. She stared at his broad back and wondered who he could be.

He can't be, surely he isn't one of them, she thought.

The man turned a little and Casey snapped her eye shut. Then the pain hit her. She clutched her abdomen and choked back a groan. She held herself for a moment with both hands and it was then that she felt the towel packed between her legs. She forgot the presence of the stranger, raised the blanket, and stared at the blood-stained towel.

"Don't move it!"

The voice snapped from across the room and Casey felt the color rise in her face.

My God! He put it there! she thought and pulled the blanket over her head. Why didn't they just kill me? I can't face this man. Oh dear God! What can I do?

"You were bleeding pretty bad. I did the best I could. How do you feel?"

Casey tried to answer. She could feel her mouth moving but words would not come. She tried again. She took a deep breath and held the blanket tight against the bed on both sides of her head.

"I don't feel very well," she said.

"I thought not. You've been unconscious for the two days that I've been here. I don't know how long before that."

Casey heard the chair scrape and the stranger exhale as he sat.

"I buried the man," he said. "Was he your husband?"

"Oh, dear God! William! William!"

Casey heard herself screaming as she threw back the cover and sat up in the bed. When she felt a hand on her shoulder, she knew it was the stranger. Someplace in the back of her mind, she wondered how he had crossed the room so fast.

The insistent hand pushed her back onto the pillow. Casey lay there and looked at the white shirt with the ruffles down the front, then forced her gaze to the man's face.

"Ma'am, I think maybe you need a doctor pretty bad."

Casey looked into his eyes and hoped the concern she read there was genuine.

"What day of the month is this?" she asked.

"I believe it's the eighteenth."

"I don't believe I need a doctor," she said.

Casey watched the tanned face turn darker as the stranger stood staring down at her.

"I'll bring in some wood," the man murmured, and turned on his heel and walked out the door.

***

Casey held onto the chair with one hand and put the food on the table with the other. She clutched the chair until the faintness left her, then tried again to cope with her feeling of shame.

I need his help but I just can't look him in the face. He knows everything, everything about me, she thought.

She started when the shadow fell across the door.

"Come in. Supper's ready," she told the shadow.

She filled both plates and stood looking at hers while the stranger took his place at the table; then she took the chair across the table from him. Casey kept her eyes on her plate or on the table and tried to eat. Occasionally, as he reached for a bowl or the plate of biscuits, she noticed the fluid movement of his slender hands.

Not like William's, she thought, and immediately felt disloyal at the comparison. Then grief surged again and she choked back the sob that seemed to be constantly in her throat.

"Mrs. Lee? Mrs. Lee?"

Casey flinched at the sound of her name and for the first time intentionally looked at Judson Wingate.

"Yes?"

"Do you think you feel well enough to go into town?"

The question caught Casey off guard and she could only stammer.

"What—what for?"

"Mrs. Lee, we should report what happened here and I imagine you might want to make some kind of arrangements—for help, or to go back to your parents, or, or—"

Casey listened to Wingate's voice trail off and suddenly she was angry with herself.

I've spent this whole week as though this man would be here to help me forever. What a fool I am! she thought. Casey put her fork on her plate.

"Of course, Mr. Wingate, perhaps we can go tomorrow."

"I thought maybe we should. Have you made any plans?"

Casey struggled for composure and wondered at her stupidity. Why haven't I been thinking about this? she wondered.

"I have thought some about it but I haven't really decided on anything," she said.

Casey felt her panic growing and tried to stop it.

"What are your plans, Mr. Wingate?"

"Jud."

"I beg your pardon?"

"Jud. Why don't you call me Jud. Everyone calls me Jud."

"All right, Mr. Wingate." Casey coughed to hide her embarrassment. "I'll call you Jud."

Casey struggled with the panic again.

"There is no reason to feel this way, Casey Lee. Just straighten yourself up," she told herself.

"What are your plans, Mr.—er—Jud?"

"Don't have any," he said.

"What is your line of work, Mr. Wingate?"

Casey watched the man across the table. He seemed to be lost in thought as he tried to balance a knife upright on its handle.

"Drifter, I guess," he said.

"You don't dress like most drifters I've seen."

The knife slipped from his fingers and he caught it before it could clatter to the table. He lowered the knife to the table and began to spin it with one finger.

"Different kind of drifter," he said.

"I don't understand."

"Mrs. Lee." He looked at her. "I'm a gambler."

Casey watched the smooth motion of his hands as he spun the knife on the table.

"Are you good at it, Jud?"

"Not lately. I ran out of aces in Waco and I've been on the run ever since."

"You mean you're wanted?"

"I'm not sure. I didn't wait to find out."

"Why do you think you're wanted if all you did was lose all your money in a poker game?"

"Well, like I said, I ran out of aces but the other fellow didn't. I had two aces and he had three. I shot him for it."

"I see. I think I understand."

Jud was silent for a moment; then he spoke.

"As a matter of fact, Mrs. Lee, you're about the only person I know that's in worse shape than I am."

Casey rose and went to the stove. She picked up the teakettle and poured hot waer into the dish pan. She waited to see if he would tell her any more.

"Did you decide to go to town tomorrow, Mrs. Lee?"

Casey turned and faced him.

"My name is Casey, Jud."

She watched his poker face slide into place.

She caught her breath as the man looked at her for a moment and she could feel a beginning change in the stranger. She had felt it from the first with William, and now in this man, she knew it was the kind of change Miss Brimley had lectured them about.

"You will learn to recognize it," Miss Brimly had said. "There is a difference that manifests itself when the situation changes from a platonic relationship to one wherein the chemistry of a man and a woman together begins to work. Watch for this and learn to deal with it."

"I want to go to town tomorrow, Jud. I'll report all this to Sheriff Billings and I want to see if I can trade William's rifle for a pistol."

Casey saw the question in just the slightest lift of Jud's eyebrows. Then she spoke, "No man is ever going to touch me again!"

CHAPTER 3

CASEY pulled as hard as she could on the strap and tried to bring the black mark on the leather through the buckle.

Why did I refuse to let him help me with this? she wondered.

The mare stood quietly and waited. Casey tried to ignore the ache in her arms, pulled harder, and watched the black mark on the strap begin to move the wrong way as she again lost her silent struggle with the mare.

She looked through the barn door and watched Jud move around the yard trying hard to look busy as he waited for her.

I guess I'll have to ask him, she thought. She looked at her small hands and, for the first time, she really understood what William had said so often. "Let me do that. Your hands are too little," he would say, and then do the task for her.

"Well, they're the only hands I've got. They will just have to do," she whispered, and reached for the strap again. This time she put her right foot against the animal's side and pulled hard. The mare settled herself on all four feet and took a breath.

The strap began to slip in Casey's hands again and she closed her eyes and pushed as hard as she could with her foot and pulled as hard as she could with her arms. Suddenly, she felt her bottom hit the straw-covered dirt floor of the barn.

Casey opened her eyes and stared at the animal's underside.

I didn't know Maude's belly was white, she thought. Casey cursed softly. "I must be losing my mind," she told herself. "What am I going to do with myself? I can't even saddle a horse."

She drew her feet up hoping the animal would not move in the stall before she could get out from under. Casey's feet tangled in her long skirt. She lay there for a moment, overwhelmed by the feeling of helplessness and paralyzed with fear by the thought of being trampled.

The mare lifted one foot and set it back in place and Casey's heart skipped a beat. Anger began to course through her.

"My God! I really am losing my mind," she murmured. "I'm lying here with my dress up to my neck and this fool animal is going to step all over me!"

"I'd be glad to saddle the mare for you, Mrs. Lee."

Casey snatched at her skirt and wiggled from under the animal.

"Oh no, you won't!" she said. "Hand me that box!"

Casey ignored Jud's puzzled look and took the small box from his hand. She carried the box into the stall and put it on the dirt floor at the mare's head. Then she lifted her skirt carefully, showing no more ankle than absolutely necessary, and stepped onto the box.

When she had both feet planted, she turned on her perch until she could look directly into the animal's left eye. The mare laid back her ears, blinked, and seemed to wait for Casey to speak.

"Maude, you and I have never particularly been friends. I didn't like you the day William brought you home and I don't like you any better now."

Casey paused to catch her breath. She hated the slow deliberate way the mare blinked her eye.

"But you are all I have, and I am all you have, and we had both better get used to that fact. Now I am going to get off this box and try to fasten that girth one more time. If you breathe in when I touch that strap, I'm going to get a piece of stove wood and beat the stuffing out of you."

Casey stepped off the box and took the strap in both hands. She held it for a moment, feeling the movement as the animal turned her head. Casey kept the strap in her hands and glared at Maude.

The mare exhaled. Casey tugged again and the buckle slipped into place.

She led the mare into the glare of the morning sunlight. As she passed Judson Wingate, her anger returned as she thought of how she had been once again exposed before this stranger.

"If you even so much as smile, I'll kill you," she said in a low voice.

At the gate Casey mounted the mare, sat erect in the saddle, and hoped she looked dignified as Jud led his red stallion through the gate and then handed her the reins. She clutched the thick leather straps and hoped the stallion would stand still while the man fastened the gate and then mounted his animal.

She touched Maude lightly with a spur and tightened her knee over the leaping hook of the sidesaddle as the animal began to move.

"I wish he would say something," she told herself. "I'd feel more comfortable somehow if he would talk. I wish I knew more about him."

When Wingate continued to ride looking straight ahead, Casey sighed and adjusted herself in the saddle and looked around her.

It's just like William said, she thought. Texas is just miles and miles of miles and miles. She let her eyes stray across the expanse of plains broken only by gulleys that years of flash floods had cut into the face of the earth.

It isn't very pretty, she thought, but still there is something about it . . .

"How far?"

"Miles and miles," Casey mused aloud; then she realized that her answer didn't make much sense.

"How far to where?" she asked.

"How far to Leedy?" he said.

"About twelve miles."

Wingate nodded, stopped his animal, and stepped from the saddle. Casey waited while the man tightened the girth.

"You have that trouble too?" she asked.

Jud looked at her and smiled.

"Every morning," he said. "I should have threatened him with stove wood, I guess."

Casey laughed and gazed at the practiced movement of his hands.

"I know I must have sounded stupid back there in the barn but I just couldn't help it. Maude exasperates me so."

"You don't really know much about life out here, do you?"

"Not much," Casey said, "but I'm learning."

Wingate mounted his animal and rode again in silence.

Casey fidgeted in the sidesaddle. She opened her mouth to speak, hesitated, then heard herself speak.

"What made you do it?"

"Do what?"

"What made you decide to be a gambler?"

Casey saw a smile tug at the corners of his mouth and then fade away.

"My hands, if anything, but I didn't really decide, it just happened."

She saw the withdrawn look cover Wingate's face.

"Jud, I'm sorry," she said. "I'm sorry I brought it up."

When there was no answer, Casey touched Maude with a spur and guided her out of the grove and back onto the narrow road.

As she rode, Casey studied the man beside her. "He's so different," she told herself. "He is just different from the others. He rides as though he is a part of his horse. Everyone else around here seems to slouch in his saddle. This man's back is as straight as a rod. He sits his horse like the gentlemen in Boston."

When Wingate pointed ahead and spoke, Casey turned her attention to him.

"Leedy?" Wingate asked.

Casey smiled.

"That's it. That's Leedy."

"Never saw anything like it."

As they came closer Casey looked at the town as though seeing it for the first time.

"It is a little different having nearly all the buildings built on one side of the street," she said.

Jud studied the town. He seems to look at things differently then most people; he's studying this town as though it is already important to him, she thought.

"What's this building closest to us that seems to sit in the middle of the street?"

"I believe that is the blacksmith shop," Casey said.

"All the buildings are on one side of the street except one," Jud observed.

"And I have no idea why. I asked William about it when we first got here and he didn't know either. He laughed at me when I said that row of buildings seems to sit all day and stare in silent disapproval at that little gun shop across the street."

Casey let her mind drift back to the day she had first seen Leedy and how she had sat high on the wagon seat and pestered William with questions about the town. When she realized that Maude had stopped and begun to graze at the side of the road, Casey glanced quickly at Jud where he sat his horse and waited. He seems to be such a patient man, Casey thought, and nudged Maude with her spurs. She rode quietly past the backsmith shop and savored the comfort of having Judson Wingate at her side.

Casey sat erect on the edge of the hard chair. Overcome

by the stifling heat and the smell of sweat in the small office, she stared at the wet patches under the fat man's arms.

He's not going to do anything, she thought. He's not capable of doing anything.

She looked away from the patches of sweat and forced her gaze to the man's face. She wished she could look at him without thinking of a pig. She looked again at his small eyes and hated the feeling that swept over her as the officer spoke.

"You wanna tell me that part again?" he asked. "The part about what they done to you?"

Casey opened her mouth to reply, then closed it again. Billings leaned forward. His lips parted and he began to breathe a little harder.

Casey clasped her hands together tightly in her lap and her voice sounded strange to her as she spoke.

"Sheriff, I have gone over it twice for you. You surely are able to understand that my husband was murdered and that I was raped."

Casey felt the rage beginning again and she rose from her seat.

"I fail to see that going over it again will help you catch these men. When do you plan to start the search?"

"Well now, Miz Lee, they's several things to be did first but I'll do my best. You can rely on that."

Casey rose to leave. At the doorway she stopped and, without turning to face him, asked, "Sheriff, do you really think you may be able to bring these men to justice?"

Her gorge rose as the odor of stale sweat surrounded her and the weight of the man's hand fell on her shoulder.

"I'll get 'em, Casey." The voice boomed in her ear.

Casey stepped to one side and the fat man's hand fell from her shoulder. She struggled for composure and spoke through gritted teeth.

"You get them, Sheriff. You get them before I do."

She put her hand to her temple and wished she could

stop the throbbing. She stepped through the door onto the wooden sidewalk.

Casey stood there for a moment, then turned and went back through the door.

"Sheriff Billings!" She faced the man. "William Lee called a man out in Abilene because that man referred to me by my given name in his presence."

Casey's stomach knotted when the fat man smiled. He wiped a trickle of tobacco juice from the corner of his mouth.

"Well, now. It just so happens that Mr. William Lee ain't just exactly available at the moment, is he now, Miz Lee?"

The sheriff completed the insult with a slow wink. Casey wished she could turn and run. Instead she backed toward the sidewalk, furious. She clamped her mouth shut on the words she wanted to shout into his slow-witted face, then turned toward the general store. She felt vulnerable and alone. She wished that someone—Jud, perhaps—would come to join her and walk by her side.

She shook her head. "Not Jud," she said to herself. "It isn't Jud I want, at all. It's William." William with the strong hands. William her lover and protector, William, who had calmly strapped on the huge gun and shot the man in Abilene for the slightest hint of rudeness.

The tears welled from under Casey's lids, blurring her vision. She wiped her eyes and strode on. She walked faster and faster, wishing she could leave the pain behind. As her strides lengthened and reached the limits of her skirt, the feel of the cloth against her legs triggered her mother's words in her mind. "Short steps, Casey. You must not stride like a man. Short steps! Always wherever you are, whatever you do, be a lady. Stand like a lady. Walk as a lady and speak as a lady. Remember!"

Casey obediently slowed her walk and pressed the handkerchief to both eyes again.

The shock of collision went through her body and for a moment she was afraid she could not hold up. Then she knew for sure that she could not. She no longer cared. It was too much. Casey let go and let her body slump.

She felt strong hands under her arms and slight pressure against her sides. She vaguely wondered who it might be. As her head began to clear a little, she opened her eyes and stared into the man's face.

Oh, God!, she thought, and her knees gave way to a new kind of weakness.

CHAPTER 4

SHE heard voices but the words seemed to have no meaning. Pain seeped through her shoulders and the small of her back as she slowly became conscious of the smell of ground coffee, brown sugar, spices, and bolts of new cloth. Then the painful stench of ammonia. Casey turned her head from side to side, fighting to stay in the comforting blackness and listen to the voices.

"Not so much, Maggie. Just enough to bring her around." And then the other voice.

"Rode into town with a stranger."

"Red McCaslin brought her in here in his arms."

"I think this one will bear watching."

Casey opened her eyes and stared at the fly-specked ceiling of Rogers's store. She lay there and wished she didn't have to face the women who surrounded her.

"Miz Lee? Are you better now? Do you know where you are?"

Casey sat up on the counter and swung her feet over the side.

"I'm better now. Thank you."

She slid from the counter and smiled at the group of women.

"I'm sorry to make such a spectacle of myself," she said. "Who brought me in here? I'd like to thank him."

No one answered her and Casey watched in amazement as the women turned away and began moving about the store. They aren't shopping, she thought. They just want to get away from me. She turned to the large woman who remained at her side.

"Did I say something wrong, Mrs. Rogers?" Casey waited while the woman studied her.

"You really don't know, do you?"

Casey shook her head and suddenly felt alone and miserable. She wished she were anywhere but here. I can't believe this, she thought. These women were friendly enough when William and I first came here. Her mother's voice rang in her head again. "Casey, men are dangerous enough but women are worse."

The voice in her ear disturbed her thoughts.

"Come into the back. Let me give you some tea and you rest for awhile," Mrs. Rogers said.

Casey didn't answer. She just followed the woman through the burlap curtain into the large storeroom.

"I've never been back here before, Mrs. Rogers." Casey surveyed the room with its boxes, bundles, and crates. Then she saw the corner, and a feeling of peace and comfort came over her.

"How lovely, Mrs. Rogers! I would never have dreamed there was anything so nice back here!"

Casey watched as the large woman moved quietly about the table with the white linen tablecloth and the delicate china tea service.

"Please have a seat. I'll fix the tea."

Casey sat primly at the table while Mrs. Rogers busied herself with a small pan of water and lit the little kerosene burner under it.

"It's my special corner. I told Mr. Rogers I just had to have it. I really need something beautiful in my life. I could not surive here if I could not cling to some tiny part of what once was."

The woman poured the boiling water in the teapot and smiled at Casey.

"Why did they turn away from me, Mrs. Rogers?"

At the woman's nod, Casey handed her cup and saucer across the table and waited for it to be filled.

"It's because you're different now. A threat, in a way."

"A threat? How could I be a threat to anyone?"

"Drink your tea."

Casey sipped the tea and studied the table.

"Mrs. Rogers, I don't understand this at all. I haven't done anything wrong. I've had a terrible thing happen to me. Now, at a time when I need help the most, you seem to be the only friend I have."

"And the man you rode in with? Is he your friend?"

Casey felt the color rise in her face. "I suppose you could say that. I don't know. He just found me and looked after me till I could get on my feet. I don't even know him, really."

She knew she had said enough but she couldn't stop the rush of words.

"He's a drifter, a gambler. I really don't know much about him. I—ah . . ."

Casey read the compassion on the older woman's face and then watched the mask of reality take its place.

"Young woman, it's time for you to grow up."

Casey shook her head as Mrs. Rogers lifted the teapot a little in a silent offer to refill her guest's cup.

"You can't expect much compassion from these women around here. They will never forgive you."

"Forgive me! Forgive me? I haven't done anything to be forgiven for."

Mrs. Rogers fished in her apron pocket and drew out a sack of tobacco and cigarette papers and calmly rolled a cigarette. She lit the cigarette and blew smoke at the ceiling.

"Of course you didn't do anything. You've had a terrible experience, but you *did* ride in here in the company of a handsome stranger a week after your husband was murdered."

Casey clenched her fists in her lap.

"I told you about that."

Mrs. Rogers puffed on the cigarette and continued, "Then you went over there and told the sheriff that you had been raped by five or six men."

"Yes, I told him what happened out there."

Mrs. Rogers puffed again on the cigarette, then ground it out in her teacup.

"They will never forgive you for being slim and beautiful."

"I never thought of myself as beautiful. Have I seemed to . . ."

Casey stopped in midsentence as Mrs. Rogers held up a hand.

"You are young. You are beautiful. You are taken care of by a handsome stranger." Casey sat stunned and tried to understand.

"And to top it all off, you were brought in here in the arms of Red McCaslin."

Casey tried to stop the trembling of her lower lip.

"For God's sake, Mrs. Rogers, who is Red McCaslin?"

Casey waited for Mrs. Rogers to answer but she only picked up the tea things and turned away from Casey. Casey rose. "Thank you, Mrs. Rogers, you have been a friend in need. I must be going now." I'm glad they've all gone, she thought as she walked through the empty store.

Out front, Casey untied the mare and led her by the reins to a small shop with a faded sign that read, Aaron Smalley—Gunsmith.

She tied the animal to the post in front of the shop and stretched to reach the whang string that held the rifle boot to the sidesaddle.

Maude lifted one foot, then the other, as she stomped at the flies.

"Stand still, Maude, before you step all over me."

Casey stretched and tugged at the leather string in an effort to untie it. As she worked, she moved closer and closer to the animal. Maude stomped again, first a hind hoof, then a front. Suddenly, Casey felt the weight of the front hoof.

Casey winced at the pain.

"Maude! Move!"

Casey released her grip on the rifle and the loosened leather string that held it. The rifle began to slip and she grabbed it to keep it in place. If I let that thing fall, Maude will jump and crush my foot, she thought.

Slowly, carefully, she began to retie the string, hoping that the mare would not shift.

As she worked, Casey felt a sudden relief from the weight that pinned her foot to the ground. I didn't feel her move—I wonder how she did that, Casey thought.

She looked down and saw only the broad back of a man squatting in the street with the mare's hoof in his hand. The man looked at Casey. His hands are strong like William's, she thought.

"Any time now, ma'am."

Casey moved her aching foot to a safe place and waited while the man released the mare's hoof and let it drop to the ground.

As he rose, Casey looked at the weathered face and wondered why it seemed so familiar.

"Thank you," she said, "I was in quite a predicament."

"Yes, ma'am."

Casey studied the somber brown eyes, then looked quickly away. She let her glance fall to the fast-draw rig on the man's hip, then back to his face.

William told me about such men, she thought. Kind to horses and children, but able to take a man's life in a lightning flash of anger.

Casey felt uncomfortable in this man's presence. I must say something, she thought.

"I'm Cas-, I'm Mrs. William Lee," she said, "and I thank you for your help."

"Yes, I know. We met on the sidewalk a little while ago. I'm Red McCaslin."

Casey hoped she wouldn't stammer this time.

"That was you? You—ah—you seem to have spent your day rescuing me one way or another. I thank you again."

Casey wondered why the man just stood there and looked at her. She wished he would leave but he continued to stand and stare. She turned and reached again for the rifle. She felt the man beside her and he had the rifle in his hand before she could stop him.

"Let me do that," he said, and handed her the weapon.

"If you will excuse me now, Mr. McCaslin, I have some business with the gunsmith."

Casey turned and started toward the shop entrance.

"Miz Lee!"

Casey stopped and spoke without turning.

"Yes."

"Miz Lee, I have something to say to you."

Casey didn't answer. She waited as if carved in place.

"Miz Lee, I want to talk to you."

"I'm listening, Mr. McCaslin. I'm listening. Yes, Mr. McCaslin, what is it you want?" Casey stood with her back to the man and waited for his answer.

"I want *you*, Mrs. Lee. I haven't been quite right in the head since you ran into me on the sidewalk."

"Whatever do you mean, Mr. McCaslin?"

Casey shuddered. A shiver spread through her shoulders and arms and down to her fingertips. She turned and looked up at the man, then away.

"What I mean is, I know you have just lost your man and all the rest of it. I'll wait long enough till it's decent and proper but then I'm going to come courting."

Casey stamped her aching foot as anger replaced the fear flooding her being and she turned to face the man.

"Mr. McCaslin!"

He was no longer in earshot and Casey watched his broad back as McCaslin crossed the dusty street.

He walks like he thinks he owns this town, she thought. No, no, that's not it at all. He walks like he doesn't give a damn who owns it. Casey sighed, then turned and walked into the gun shop with the rifle in her hand.

"I probably should have shot him," she muttered.

CHAPTER 5

THE man behind the counter looked up and waited till
Casey put the rifle down before him; then he spoke.

"You're Miz Lee, aren't you?"

"Yes."

"I met your man. Did some work on that rifle for him
right after you all got here. Is it broken again?"

Casey shook her head.

"No, Mr. Smalley. I want to trade it. I need a handgun."

Casey stood on her good foot and stared at the
gunsmith. He opened his mouth, then closed it without
speaking. He picked up the rifle and worked the lever
several times. Casey tapped her fingers on the counter and
waited for the man to finish the inspection. Finally he put
the rifle back on the counter.

"A derringer for your purse, I suppose?"

"No. Something heavier than that and I want the thing
to have a hair trigger."

Casey tried to shift her shoulders a little while a drop of
perspiration rolled down between her shoulder blades,
and she realized Smalley was speaking to her again.

"Miz Lee, do you know what a hair trigger is?"

"I think I do. William told me that such a weapon is very
easy to fire. He used one once in Abilene."

"Yes'm. That is exactly right. About all you have to do
with a hair-triggered weapon is to hold it in your hand and
think about it and the thing will go off."

Casey drew her shoulders forward as slightly as she could and felt the relief as the cloth on her back soaked up the drop of perspiration. The pain throbbed in her foot again and she wondered if the foot was beginning to swell. She thought, Why do men have to talk forever about the simplest things?

"Mr. Smalley, do you have such a weapon that you are willing to trade?"

Casey waited while Smalley reached into the case, brought out a pistol, and placed it on a piece of velvet on the countertop. Casey shook her head. "It looks too small," she said. "I want a big one, like the men wear."

"Miz Lee, this is a thirty-eight-caliber pistol. It holds six shots and is what we call double action. That means that it will shoot six times if you keep pulling the trigger."

Casey waited while the man paused and seemed to study her for a moment.

"Ma'am, a weapon doesn't have to be large to be deadly. Handguns are for short-range work and size really doesn't mean much close up."

Casey wiggled her toes and tried to ease the pain in her foot. He's going to go on about this forever, she thought, and tried to force her mind back to the stream of words from the gunsmith: "Very few men are accurate with those big weapons they wear. Oh, they look good and they make a lot of noise and there's a lot of flash when they are fired. But those big weapons also jump around and it takes quite a while to get them back on target. Sometimes that can be important. Believe me, Miz Lee, if you are determined to have a handgun, this would be better."

Casey took the gun in her hand and hefted it. She liked the feel of the weapon. She cocked the hammer back and sighted down the barrel, hoping she looked as though she knew something about what she was doing.

"I hope it's not loaded," she said; then she felt the hammer fall on the empty chamber.

"Did I do that?" she asked.

The gunsmith didn't answer. Casey looked at the worry line that appeared above the man's eyes. "He thinks I can't handle it," she told herself. She put the gun back on the counter.

"Will you trade it for the rifle, Mr. Smalley? I'll need the pistol, ammunition, and a holster."

"All for one rifle?"

"You get the rifle boot too."

"Miz Lee, you're not thinking of *wearing* this thing, are you? No lady in this town . . ."

"Mr. Smalley, do we have a trade or not?"

Casey held her breath and waited for the answer.

"Yes, ma'am, we do."

Casey drummed on the counter again while the man fitted the gun into a holster, slid the holster onto a belt, and then turned and took boxes of ammunition from the shelf behind him. He placed it all on the counter before her.

"Here you are, Mrs. Lee. Even trade."

Casey nodded, slung the belt over her shoulder, picked up the ammunition, and walked out the door. Outside, Maude stepped sideways as Casey draped the gun rig over the sidesaddle.

"Stand still, fool!" Casey scolded. She touched the pommel of the sidesaddle and looked both ways; then she untied the animal and limped down the street toward the livery stable.

I'll bet I have trouble with this, Casey thought. I've heard about horse traders. She stopped in front of the barn, tied Maude to the rail, and waited.

I'll stay out here till someone comes out, she thought . . . wouldn't want someone to steal the pistol.

Casey waited in the sun. Minutes passed and no one came or went. She peered into the dark interior of the barn. Looks cool in there, she thought.

Casey reached for the pistol. "Well, Maude, I can't stay out here forever." She lifted the pistol from its holster, patted Maude, and stepped into the doorway of the barn. She stood for a moment waiting for her eyes to adjust to the darkness.

"You figgerin' on robbin' this livery stable, lady?"

Casey jumped at the sound of the voice behind her and she felt the pistol click in her hand as she turned to face the huge man.

"Do you run this place?"

"Yes'm. It and the blacksmith shop. Most everybody knows where to find me and they just come on over there. This is the first time I have had to come over here to get robbed."

"I'm not going to rob anybody. I want to trade my saddle."

Casey pointed to Maude standing in the sun with her head down.

"I don't have much use for a sidesaddle," the man said. "It's mostly men that rents from me."

"Well, I have to have another saddle. A regular one. One like men ride."

Casey waited while the man turned and faced her.

"I've got what you want, all right, but I'll have to have some boot."

Casey's heart began to beat a little faster.

"Boot? How much boot?" she asked.

"Five dollars."

Casey studied the man's face and decided he had made a take-it-or-leave-it offer. Oh, God! Where will I get five dollars, she thought. She wrinkled her nose and smiled the way William had liked.

"That will be just fine. Just put the saddle on my mare. I'm Mrs. William Lee. We haven't been here long but we have credit at the store. You can just put the five dollars on your books and . . ."

When the man held up his hand, it seemed to be the only thing Casey could see. She looked at the hand while the man spoke one word. "Cash!"

Casey felt color burn her face.

"I see. You only deal in cash. Well, I believe I'll just look around town and see if I can find a better trade."

Casey turned and limped toward the door. Now a trickle of sweat ran down between her breasts and she longed to claw at it as the sound of her mother's voice sounded in her head.

"Casey, one never touches one's body in public. One must always stand erect. A lady never fidgets."

Once again Casey jumped at the sound of a voice behind her.

"Sold! Change the saddle for the lady."

Casey whirled, and before she could stop it, the thought burst from her lips.

"Judson Wingate! You fool! Where would you get five dollars?"

She watched in astonishment as Wingate counted out the silver dollars from a stack in his hand. Then she limped back into the barn and waited beside Jud while the saddles were changed.

"Jud, where did you get all that money?"

Jud reached for the pistol Casey still carried in her hand. He examined it carefully before he answered.

"Met a fellow who thought he could play poker. Fellow by the name of Red McCaslin," he said.

CHAPTER 6

CASEY tried to stifle a feeling of irritation at the mention of Red McCaslin's name. I've heard enough of him for one day, she thought. I hope I don't have to hear any more about him for a long time.

Casey took her weapon as Jud handed it back to her.

"Nice weapon. Know how to use it?" he asked.

"I'll learn."

"You know it's dangerous?"

Casey recognized Jud's words as half statement, half question. She limped to Maude and put the pistol in the saddlebag along with the holster and extra ammunition.

"That a fast-draw saddlebag you got there?"

Casey turned and faced Jud and the mockery in his eyes.

"Mr. Wingate, I have no intention of attempting to draw and fire my pistol from a saddlebag. I shall take the thing home and practice with it until I am proficient. Then when I need it, I shall use it. Is there anything else you would like to know?"

"Yes. I need to know whether you plan to go home soon or do you plan to spend the night in town?"

"I plan to go home whenever you are ready."

Casey tried to control her panic as she listened to Jud's words.

"Mrs. Lee, I plan to leave town tomorrow. I can't ride back to your place with you. I'm going the other direction."

I knew that, she thought. Why can't I use some common

sense? This man has done all for me that he is willing to do. She looked at Wingate and smiled.

"I'm sorry, Mr. Wingate. I do not wish to impose upon you further. I simply forgot for a moment."

She extended her hand and waited for Wingate to take it in his.

"I want to thank you for everything you have done for me and I want to wish you the best," she said.

Casey stood with her hand in Jud's and wondered why she was somehow surprised at the strength she felt in the man. She saw no mockery in his eyes now as she waited for him to speak. When he said nothing, she disengaged her hand and said, "Was there anything else, Jud?" Casey looked directly into Jud's eyes as she spoke. She stared and almost gasped. I think I know what the gambler in Waco saw, she thought.

"There is one more thing, Mrs. Lee. You are not to leave this town in possession of that weapon without knowing something about how to use it. I will not permit you to do that."

Casey felt the force in this man's voice as though it were a physical touch.

"I want you to come with me now and learn something about how to use the thing."

Casey formed the words in her mind to refuse; then she looked at Jud's face again.

"I think I will," she said, and turned and walked to her mare.

Jud picked up the wooden mounting box and set it beside the animal and disappeared into the barn. Casey stepped onto the box, put her left foot in the stirrup, and hooked her right leg over the saddle horn just as she had always done with the sidesaddle.

It's not very comfortable but it will do till I can get out of sight, she thought. Then I can ride astride, and if I show some leg, he will just have to look the other way.

Jud appeared in the doorway of the barn already

mounted on the red stallion. Casey felt the trembling in Maude and leaned forward to growl in the mare's ear.

"Don't be silly, Maude! That is the same horse we rode in with!"

Casey paused; then as an afterthought, she murmured, "He's leaving town anyway."

She patted the mare on the neck and waited for her to settle down. Then Casey reined the animal about and rode after Jud Wingate.

Casey rode beside Jud in silence and waited for some sign from the man as to what was expected of her. Her right leg began to ache from the pressure of the pommel of the saddle against her. Her seat was damp with perspiration. I can learn about that silly pistol by myself, she thought. Why doesn't he just ride on back to town?

Suddenly the pain in the right leg was too much for her and she reined Maude to a stop. She sat for a moment. I've either got to get off this horse, or I've got to lift my right leg high over Maude's neck. Casey leaned back in the saddle and lifted her right foot over the animal's neck and put her foot in the right stirrup. "That's better!" she breathed as she pushed the skirt and petticoats down as far as they would go, and welcomed the relief of the breeze on her legs.

Casey kicked Maude into a trot and they caught up with Jud and the red stallion. She blushed as Jud glanced at her, then quickly glanced away again.

She worked Maude into the mare's best gait and settled herself to listen to the creak of the saddle leather and to watch the little puffs of dust rise around the stallion's hoofs.

I wonder what William would want me to do, she mused. If he could only tell me one little thing. I'll probably have to sell everything. I don't see how I can stay there very long. I wonder if we owe money? I think William paid cash for the place. I wish he had told me more.

The angry buzzing sound on the ground and Maude's

terrified leap sent a shock through Casey's body. She jerked at the reins and felt one heavy leather strip slip through her fingers. The sound of Jud's pistol sounded through the confusion as she fought the mare and her skirt. She could see the stallion jumping too as Wingate fired from the saddle.

She worked the mare in a circle with the one rein. "A circle will keep her from running" ran through Casey's mind. Then she patted Maude as the horse stepped sideways time after time and then stopped and stood trembling. Casey didn't move. She sat perfectly still with her eyes closed and listened to her mother's words in her mind, "Under stress, breathe slowly, my dear. It helps one maintain one's composure."

Casey heard the dancing footsteps of the stallion beside her and still she sat with her eyes closed and pulled the dusty air in and out.

She sensed the movement of Jud Wingate's body as he leaned from his saddle to recover the lost rein. Then she felt the light brush of the back of his hand on her bare leg as he brought the rein up to within her grasp. A rush of anger flooded Casey at the touch and she snapped her eyes open. Her gaze moved to her skirt high above her knees. She tugged at the skirt again. He didn't mean to touch me, she thought.

"Rattler," Jud said, as he handed her the rein.

"You killed it?"

Jud nodded.

Casey heard the tone of her voice rising, and she wished she could be calm, but she knew she couldn't.

"From the back of a plunging horse, you shot that snake? Just like that, you shot it?"

Jud nodded again. "He's over there. You want to see it?"

"Lord, no! I hope I never see another snake as long as I live!"

"You will," Jud said. "Let's ride on a little way and let the horses settle; then we'll work with your pistol."

Casey nodded and touched her spurs to Maude's ribs. She rode awhile before she spoke.

"Jud, can you teach me that?"

"Teach you what?"

"To shoot like that. Fast and accurate and all of it."

Jud frowned and shook his head.

"Not in a hurry," he said.

Casey watched his frown deepen.

"Are you planning something, Mrs. Lee?"

Casey hesitated for a moment before she answered.

"Just to learn to use my weapon. You will teach me to handle a gun like you do, won't you Jud? Do you really have to ride on? You could stay long enough for that, couldn't you?"

Wingate held up his right hand, flexed his fingers, and looked at them for a moment.

"When I was very small, I knew there was something special about my hands," he said. "I could do things the other boys couldn't do: untie a knot in a piece of thread, catch a fly in flight . . . ."

"That must have been fun," Casey said.

"It was, in a way, but it worried me some. It made me different and that wasn't always easy."

"Do you have to have good hands to be a gambler?"

Casey saw the smile tugging again and she smiled a little too.

"Sometimes it helps," he said.

"Well, did you just grow up and one day say to yourself, 'I have these wonderful hands so I will learn to shoot and to be a gambler?'"

"Not quite. My father was the captain of the *Delta Star* out of New Orleans. The boat was a river steamer and he spent most of his time on the boat going up the Mississippi and back again. She was a fine ship and he was proud to be captain. Mother and I stayed in New Orleans and he spent as much time as he could with us but, for my mother, it was still a lonely life."

He paused and then added, "I learned it on the boat."

Casey looked at the man.

"I beg your pardon?"

"I learned it on the boat. The gambling, I mean. When my father took me to live on the boat, gambling seemed to be something everybody did. Everybody gambled. The passengers, the deckhands, the waiters, all of them. Gambling was a way of life on the *Delta Star*."

"It sounds exciting," Casey said as she shifted in the saddle and urged Maude a little closer to the other animal.

"Exciting? Maybe, but it didn't seem that way to me then. It was just something to do. I usually lost until Colonel Potter took me in hand."

"Colonel Potter?"

"Yes, he was a professional gambler who always rode the *Delta Star*. He ran a nightly poker game in his stateroom."

Casey squirmed in her saddle again.

"I'm not used to these long rides," she said. "When we reach the grove, I'd like to step down and rest for a few minutes."

Wingate nodded and rode in silence.

When they reached the small grove of trees, Casey guided Maude into the shade and dismounted. She stood by her animal and lifted one foot and then the other to relieve the stiffness in her limbs.

Wingate leaned against the red stallion and waited.

"Tell me about Colonel Potter," Casey said.

"He wasn't much different than any other riverboat gambler, I guess, but I thought he was wonderful."

Jud moved toward her then. Without thinking, Casey shrank back against Maude. Wingate stopped and looked at her, then smiled.

"Please don't be afraid of me. I only wanted to check your saddle girth."

Casey moved away and heard her own whisper.

"I'm sorry."

She watched his hands as he worked with the girth. Not

at all like William's, she thought, then felt the surge of grief once again as she realized that William was gone. I must not offend this man again, she thought. He has been nothing but careful and gracious with me. A real gentleman.

"Did Colonel Potter teach you to gamble then?"

When Wingate turned to her, he seemed relieved to return to the conversation and spoke as he helped her mount Maude.

"Yes, and it was fun, although I'm sure I didn't fully understand everything he said . . . and he nearly scared me to death the first time we met."

Casey looked sharply at him.

"Oh?"

Wingate laughed and Casey could see that Jud had fond memories of the man.

"Yes, we were standing near each other at the rail one afternoon and I caught a fly on the wing. He saw me do it and moved closer. 'Let's see you do that again,' he said. When I did it again, he grabbed my hands and looked at them carefully and then said, 'Come with me,' and dragged me down the deck to his cabin."

"Good heavens! You must have been frightened."

"I was at first, but when he took me in his cabin and showed me card tricks, it began to be fun. I spent hours with him every day and enjoyed every bit of it. He taught me how to handle every kind of poker hand and, I realized later, every possible way to manipulate a deck of cards. He never mentioned cheating. Sometimes, if I didn't handle the cards well, he would be angry with me and end the session for the day."

Casey looked at the man at her side.

"He taught you all that and you were only a child? He sounds like a terrible man."

Casey saw the look of sadness return and she waited for him to speak again.

"No, he was a wonderful man. He was more of a father than my own father. He disappeared the night the *Delta Star* sank. I lost my father and Colonel Potter both that night."

"What happened?" Casey asked breathlessly.

"A drunken wheelman made a wrong turn in the river and ripped her hull. She went down in minutes. I was in Potter's cabin watching the game. We went over the side together. It was dark in that water and the current was strong but Potter was near me. The last I saw of him, he pushed a piece of debris toward me, waved, and then swam away."

Jud looked wistful for a few moments. Then he reined up, turned in the saddle, and looked at her.

"Anyway, Mrs. Lee, I really would like to stay on, but you know what people would say and . . ."

Casey heard her mother again: ". . . and like Caesar's wife, you must avoid even the appearance of . . ."

Suddenly frustration overwhelmed her consideration for the story he'd told; she straightened in the saddle and said, "Jud Wingate! You come home with me!"

She leaned forward in the saddle, pushed the reins as close to Maude's ears as she could get them, and touched the animal in the ribs again and again with both spurs.

As she rode without a backward look, the memory of the things he'd revealed and the feel of the back of Jud's hand against her thigh returned.

Casey smiled and let the wind wash over her face.

CHAPTER 7

CASEY moved the lamp closer and studied the skirt. She smoothed it with the palms of her hands until the garment lay flat on the table. Then she moved around the table and studied it from another angle and recalled the afternoon of practice with Jud.

"You're doing better. Your shooting is accurate now, but . . ."

"But what, Jud? What am I doing wrong?"

"Well, you know about the hair-trigger problem. You're still getting one in the dirt, then one in the target, but that's not all . . ."

"Jud, tell me! Tell me what it is!"

"I have to tell you, I don't see how you are ever going to get fast . . . not the way things are and all."

"Jud, you're fast! You can teach me that, too. I know I'm smart enough to learn it."

"Not in that skirt, I can't."

"Why?"

"Haven't you noticed that every time you draw your gun that holster moves around a little, and from that point on, it is really in the way?"

"Yes, of course I'd noticed it, but I thought you would tell me later what to do about it."

"To get really fast and to keep from getting that first shot into the ground, that holster needs to be tied to your, ah—limb."

Casey moved around the table and studied the skirt

some more. I suppose I could put a small hole in the front and one in the back, she thought. Then she shook her head, picked up the lamp, went to the bedroom, and began to peel the layers of clothing from her body. First the skirt, then the petticoats. Casey pulled the cotton gown on over her head and stood for a moment looking at the shaft of lantern light that shone through a crack of the barn.

She sighed, turned away from the window, and sank into bed. "He's still awake," she whispered into the darkness.

Casey lay on her back and felt the emptiness of William's side of the bed. Then she reached under his pillow for the unwashed shirt and buried her face in it. She breathed the odor of William's body and did the little thing she had always done before.

Casey moved her foot slowly toward William's side of the bed and let the happy anticipation of the feel of his bare foot flow through her. When the shock of the emptiness struck her again, she lay and sobbed into the shirt. "William! William! Why?"

Casey turned on her side and held the shirt close for a long time. She kissed it tenderly and hugged it closer a little longer, then rose and made her way through the darkness to the corner of the room.

"Goodbye, my darling," she said, and carefully tucked the shirt into the basket of dirty laundry.

Casey felt her way back to the bedside table and lit the lamp. She carried the lamp to the shelf and took down her sewing basket and went to the kitchen. She put the lamp on the table and felt in the basket until she found her scissors.

Casey folded the skirt lengthwise and cut along the fold about half its length. Then she held the skirt up to herself, put it back on the table, and cut a little further. She turned the split skirt inside out, threaded a needle, and listened to her mother's words as she stitched the inseam of her new garment: "Make the stitches small, Casey. Very small. Only a slovenly woman would use large stitches. It is evidence of your skill and perhaps someday will be evidence of your love."

Casey held up the work and looked at it.

"This should let me tie that thing to my 'ah, limb,'" she muttered. Casey smiled at the thought of Jud's shyness, then glanced at the early morning light framed by the kitchen window and put the skirt aside.

Time to start breakfast, she thought, and reached into the wood box for kindling wood.

Casey turned the pan of biscuits onto the plate, put the plate in the warming oven, stepped to the doorway again, and looked toward the barn.

He's late this morning. I've never had to hold breakfast for him before. Casey stood in the doorway and wondered whether she should call out to Jud or go down to the barn to see about him. She turned and went back to the stove. She opened the warming oven again and looked, first at the plate of biscuits and then over her shoulder at the table. I wish he *would* come on while this food is still fit to eat, she thought.

She wandered to the bedroom and picked up her night's work and held it up before her.

"Why am I looking at this fool thing again? I know it will work," she muttered.

She threw the garment on the bed and strode out of the bedroom through the kitchen, out the door, and down to the barn.

"Jud! Jud? Are you all right?"

The uneasy stillness of the barn seeped into Casey and she felt the weakness begin in her legs as she started up the ladder to the loft.

Beams of sunlight from the cracks of the barn sliced the darkness of the loft and blinded her for a moment. Casey shaded her eyes with one hand and searched the loft for Jud.

First she saw the depression in the straw where he had

slept; then she saw the scrap of paper. Casey scruffed through the straw on the floor and snatched up the note. She stepped closer to the wall and read the message by one of the shafts of sunlight. As she read, the manure and urine smell of the barn swept over her and she retched as she sank to her knees in the straw.

Casey sat for a long time and watched the dust motes dance in the streaks of sunlight. Then she climbed down the ladder and walked slowly to the house. Inside she lifted the cap from the top of the stove. She held the note for a moment, then she put it on the coals and watched as it turned brown and then burst into flame.

Casey sat at the table and forced herself to eat. When she had finished, she cleared the table and washed the dishes. I must do something. Something definite, she thought. He is gone now and there is nothing to be done about that. I must do it all myself now.

Casey rose and went to the bedroom and brought back her pistol and holster. She took the pistol from the holster and unloaded it, letting the shells fall slowly onto the table one by one. Then she put the pistol beside the shells and picked up the holster and examined it. She strapped it on and examined it again. "I need a whang string to hold it down," she said, and walked out the door and down to the barn again.

Maude stomped and moved around in her stall. Casey ignored the sounds and pawed through William's big box of leather tools. Maude snorted and moved restlessly again. Those flies must be driving her crazy, Casey thought. I'd better look at her.

She found the roll of leather scraps and felt in the corners of the box for the leather punch. She stuffed the punch into the end of the roll of leather and leaned further into the large box to see if there was anything else that she might need.

When Casey heard the growl, she froze. She stayed where she was with her head in the box and stopped breathing and listened. There is a *dog* in here, she thought. I didn't know there was a dog within miles. Casey wanted to move but fear held her motionless. She let her breath out slowly and listened for movement behind her. Me and my big pistol, she thought. It's lying up there on that table unloaded and I'm down here all bent over and afraid to straighten up.

Casey listened as Maude shifted and snorted and stomped her feet again. Casey took a deep breath and straightened herself. "Who's there?" she asked without turning. She reached slowly into the roll of leather for the punch and waited for an answer.

When Maude's hoof hit the side of the stall hard, Casey whirled and raised the punch high over her head, ready to strike.

"For heaven's sake!" she said aloud as she stared into the yellow eyes of a red dog. "That dog is looking over the top of that stall."

Casey backed away until she felt her heels against the big wooden box behind her. It looks friendly enough, she thought, but where could it have come from?

"Well, I can't just stand here all day," she murmured to herself. Casey moved slowly at first as she worked her way around the stall divider. Then she stood stunned at the sight of the dog perched on Maude's rump. It faced backward, shifting easily from time to time to maintain her balance as the mare moved about in the stall.

Casey let relief flow through her at the sight and welcomed the hysterical laughter that overwhelmed her. When she could laugh no longer, she balled her fists, put them on her hips, and tried to make her voice sound stern.

"Stranger, get off my horse!"

She waited while the dog hesitated, then jumped to the floor of the barn and came to her with tail wagging. Casey carefully reached out and patted the red head. As Casey patted the dog, its golden eyes seemed to her to plead for acceptance. She stuffed the punch back into the end of the roll of leather and started for the door.

"All right. Come on to the house and you can have Jud's biscuits."

As the red dog ran ahead of her, Casey studied the animal. She's not a big dog, but she's not little, either, she thought. I wonder whatever possessed her to get up on Maude that way?

Casey emptied the plate of biscuits on the porch before the dog and went back into the kitchen. She picked up the roll of leather and tugged at the leather string that held the bundle together. This knot won't move, she thought, and reached for a fork. She tried to force a tine of the fork through the outside loop of the knot. Casey felt the sudden release of knot and the pain as the tine jabbed her thumb.

"Damn! Why would he tie that thing so tight?"

Casey jammed her thumb into her mouth and sank slowly into a chair.

The nudge of the wet nose against her leg brought her to reality again and Casey reached down and slowly stroked the animal's head.

"Stranger, we're not as poor as I thought we were," she said.

CHAPTER 8

CASEY led Maude from the barn to the watering trough and waited for the animal to drink. She patted the pocket where she had pinned her money and glanced toward the house to be sure she had closed the door. She felt the mare flinch and she turned to see why.

"Stranger! What are you doing up there again? You know how Maude hates that."

When the red dog flattened herself against the horse and put her chin on her front feet, Casey sighed.

"Oh well, all right, you can ride part of the way but you will have to get off before we get to town. I'm not going to ride in looking silly."

Casey mounted the mare, touched her lightly with a spur, and settled into the saddle as Maude moved off at a walk.

I hope we don't meet anyone, and if we do, I hope Stranger doesn't sit straight up and call attention to herself the way she usually does, Casey thought. Casey urged Maude to her one good gait and shifted the gun belt to a more comfortable position. She smiled and shook her head as she felt the dog sit up. "Well, here goes the circus," she said aloud, and shifted in the saddle again.

Casey liked the fit of the new split skirt and the feel of the tied-down holster. I feel safer now, she thought.

At the edge of town, she brought Maude to a halt, twisted, and spoke to the dog's back.

"All right, Stranger. Get off my horse."

She waited while the dog bounded to the ground and sat looking up at her.

"Just follow along like everybody else's dog does. It won't hurt you a bit."

Casey smiled as Stranger wagged her tail, then settled into a trot beside the mare. The dog hung her head and let her tongue loll out of her mouth. She's trying to look like a dog that has run ten miles in the heat, Casey thought.

Casey rode down the middle of the empty street and stopped at the blacksmith shop and read the peeling sign: "Wilford E. Buck, Blacksmith."

"Maude, this town could use a sign painter. I wish I knew how to do something like that."

"Need something, Miz Lee? Mare throw a shoe? What can I do for you?"

Casey put her weight in the left stirrup and swung herself off Maude.

"I'm here to talk business with you, Mr. Buck," she said.

"Yes, ma'am, that's what I asked you about."

"You don't understand, Mr. Buck. I don't need any blacksmith work."

"Well, that's the business I'm in here. I don't know what else . . ."

Casey moved away from Maude and came face to face with the huge man. She rested her hand on her gun butt and wondered why the corners of his mouth began to turn up.

"Did you decide to come back and rob me after all?"

"No! Of course I'm not here to rob anyone."

"Well, Miz Lee, every time I see you, you've got that gun in your hand or you want credit or something. You make me kind of nervous."

"Keep an eye on her, Buck! She looks dangerous to me!" The voice came from inside the blacksmith shop.

Casey fought back anger as she spoke.

"Who's the smart aleck?" she asked.

Buck looked over his shoulder, then back at Casey.

"That there is Mr. Red McCaslin," he said. "I'm shoeing his horse."

Casey whirled and stomped to Maude's side and reached for the saddle horn. She frowned when Buck reached for the mare's bridle; then she realized that his gesture was an automatic act of courtesy. Casey climbed into the saddle and turned to the blacksmith.

"Mr. Buck, if you think you might find some time later in the day . . .," she glanced toward the shop, "when we could talk privately, I would appreciate it."

Buck sorted Maude's mane with his thick fingers.

"I ain't gonna be doing nothing around noon," he said. "That's when I eat my dinner."

Casey kicked the mare and looked over her shoulder to see if Stranger was following. Then she guided Maude down the street to Rogers's store. Inside, she saw no one and she walked towards the back door.

Casey started at the sound of a voice; then, without thinking, she turned and dropped her hand to her gun butt. For a tense moment, the two women stared at each other; then the older woman smiled.

"You look shifty and dangerous today, Casey. How long have you been wearing that thing?"

"Not very long, but I do know how to use it. Where did you come from? I looked all around when I came in. I was hoping you'd be having tea."

"I was bent over behind the counter. I could tell by the sound that you were going toward the back and that I had time to finish what I was doing and still not lose a customer."

Casey relaxed, took her hand away from her gun, and tugged the list of supplies from under her gun belt. She handed Mrs. Rogers the list.

"I need a few things. Can you put them in a sack that I can tie to the saddle horn?"

Casey moved to the counter and thumbed the pages of a catalogue while she waited. When Mrs. Rogers began to write a charge ticket, Casey stopped her.

"I'll pay cash for this, and if you'll figure up my bill, I'll pay that too."

Casey tapped her toe and scanned the catalogue while Mrs. Rogers figured. She glanced up sharply when the older woman snorted, then laughed out loud.

"What's so funny, Mrs. Rogers?"

"Don't mind me, dear. I just thought of something that struck me as funny."

"Tell me."

"Well, Mr. Rogers always offers the gentlemen a cigar when they pay their bill. I was about to offer you a cup of tea."

She paused and looked Casey up and down. "Or would you rather have the cigar?" she asked.

Casey smiled. "I haven't taken up cigars yet and I would love a cup of your tea."

Mrs. Rogers jerked her head toward the back, then followed her own gesture. She stopped at the door and held the curtain aside for Casey. Casey entered and went directly to the table and seated herself in the chair she had used before. She took the cup of tea as her mother's words came into her mind: "One ordinarily waits for an older person to begin a conversation, Casey."

She sipped the tea and waited. The older woman did not speak, but simply sat and looked at her over the rim of the teacup. Casey knew by the vacant look in the woman's eyes that Mrs. Rogers's mind was at some other tea table in some other time. Casey waited a little longer; then she spoke.

"How have you been, Mrs. Rogers?"

Casey waited while Mrs. Rogers brought herself back to the present.

"Oh! Very well, but busy. I'm alone here today. Mr. Rogers has gone down the street to have a drink with a drummer that wants to sell him something new. The man called it barbed wire, I think. I don't suppose Rogers will buy it, though." Then Mrs. Rogers looked into her teacup and said quietly, "I hope he doesn't stay all day."

"Barbed wire," Casey murmured. Then she sat silently while Mrs. Rogers seemed to shake herself a little. The older woman reached into her apron for tobacco and cigarette papers. Casey said nothing while the woman rolled the cigarette, lit it, and pulled the smoke into her lungs.

"Casey, what the hell are you up to?"

The sudden harsh question shocked her and Casey could only stammer. "Whatever do you mean, Mrs. Rogers?"

"Don't give me any of that finishing-school rhetoric. I went to one of those, too."

Casey felt the color flood her face and she wished she didn't feel the need to defend herself.

"What is all this with the split skirt and the tied-down fast-draw rig? Haven't you been talked about enough already?"

Casey felt her anger rise and she liked the feeling of strength that came with it. She listened to the words as they came from her mouth and she was sure that it was all new to her.

"Mrs. Rogers, you are probably the only friend I have in this town and I want to keep your friendship. But what I do will have to be whatever I think is best. I happen to think that I am dressed the way I need to be. I feel safer with the gun and I intend to wear it."

Casey rose, leaned over the table, and shook her finger in Mrs. Rogers's face.

"Men have the best of everything! They wear guns and they take whatever they want. Well, I am not going to have it that way any longer. I am going to wear this gun the rest of my life and no man is ever going to touch me again!"

Casey stopped and stood shaking, then sank into her chair trying to remember all that she had said.

Mrs. Rogers filled the cups again and Casey left hers sitting in the saucer.

"Bravo! Casey, but I'm not so sure that will all work out that way for you. Especially that last part. There is already one man that is dead set to have you. He was here yesterday wanting me to put in a good word for him."

Casey reached for the cup and hoped it wouldn't rattle against the saucer when she picked it up. When the cup rattled, she tried to cover the sound with a question.

"Am I supposed to ask who the man is, Mrs. Rogers?"

"I think you know who, Casey, and you'd do well to think about it."

Casey rose. "Thank you for the tea, Mrs. Rogers. I must go. I have an appointment at noon." Casey moved to the door. I really wish I could talk to her about my plan, Casey thought, but she would never understand.

Casey put her hand on the curtain, hesitated, and then turned back.

"Mrs. Rogers, please. Just who is this Red McCaslin?"

"That's something I sure would like to talk to you about, ma'am."

Casey spun on her heel at the sound of the man's voice behind her. Suddenly everything was a tangle of curtains, the feel of a rough shirt against her face, strong arms tightening around her, and the pain of a belt buckle that pressed against her body.

She pushed against the man and felt his arms relax. Casey stepped back and looked up into the weathered face of Red McCaslin. He held the curtain to one side and smiled down at Casey.

She stood mute and fought the tiny tingle of unwanted passion and silently cursed herself, then pushed past the watching man. Casey moved to the hitching post in a blur. When she mounted Maude, Stranger jumped to the back of the horse and rode the length of the street. Casey didn't speak to the dog. Minutes passed while she waited for the blacksmith.

Casey stood quietly beside the anvil and waited for Buck to finish with the horseshoe. He hit the shoe one more time with his hammer and then dropped it sizzling into a tub of water. She watched the little cloud of steam rise and wondered if she should have come back here at all.

"Mr. Buck."

"Just Buck," the man said. "Just call me Buck."

"I'm sorry to bother you when you are so busy but you did say to come back at noon."

"It's fine, ma'am, I was just about to stop and eat my dinner."

He reached for a flour sack on the workbench behind him and took out a huge sandwich. Casey wondered if he could really eat it all. She shook her head when he broke the sandwich in two and offered her half.

"Please go ahead and eat, Mr. Buck. Don't mind me."

Casey watched in fascination as the man began a methodical destruction of the sandwich.

"What can I do for you, Miz Lee?"

Casey choked and she felt her heart pound as she tried to speak.

"How . . . how would you like to sell me the livery stable?"

Casey waited for the man to speak but he only looked at her and chewed. I wonder if he understood me, she thought. He doesn't look very bright. Casey looked out the door while she waited for Buck to speak. She saw Stranger mount herself on Maude and sit looking proudly down the street. Casey turned back to the man. He swallowed.

"Horses, too?" he asked.

"No. I don't need the horses. You could keep them. I only need the building."

"Where?"

"Where, what?" Casey asked.

He's just not following this, she thought, and Stranger looks like such a fool perched up there.

"Where would I keep the horses?"

"You could build a shed behind the shop here."

Casey held her breath while the man furrowed his brow and began to shake his head slowly.

"Then you wouldn't have to go back to the stable every time someone wants to rent a horse."

Casey could hear Maude beginning to move and stomp her feet.

"Don't seem like no proper way to run a livery," Buck said.

"Buck, wouldn't you be better off with four hundred dollars? . . ." She turned her head and snapped over her shoulder, "Stranger! Get down off of Maude." Casey turned back to the blacksmith, "Than you would be with that old barn?"

"Four fifty," he said.

Casey extended her hand and felt the huge paw swallow it.

"Done!" she said.

"Cash," Buck said.

Casey nodded. "Your favorite word."

"I'll have the justice of the peace draw up the papers, Miz Lee. You can take possession the end of the week."

Casey nodded, shook hands again, and walked out the door. She mounted Maude and looked around for Stranger. The dog followed as Casey started Maude down the street. Casey stopped then, turned Maude, and rode back to the blacksmith shop. She leaned in the saddle and peered through the door. "Buck! Buck!" she called. The big man came to the door.

"Yes, Miz Lee?"

"Buck, what is barbed wire?" Casey asked.

CHAPTER 9

"STRANGER, you can just walk till we get out of town. You may not care how we look, but I do."

At the edge of town, Casey urged Maude into her comfortable gait and settled herself for the long ride home. The late-afternoon sun felt good on her back at first, then uncomfortable, then miserable. She shrugged and shifted in the saddle. The discomfort from the heat and an ache in her left leg grew and grew. I believe this left stirrup strap is longer than the other. She looked down at the strap. I'll stop at the grove and see if I can do anything about it. Sweat prickled beneath her breasts. I need to get in the shade for a while anyway.

She slid to one side in the saddle and stood in the right stirrup to ease her pain. I'll just let Maude plod along here, and when we leave the grove, I can let Stranger ride, she thought.

Casey watched Stranger ranging back and forth, and when she came near again, she spoke to the dog.

"Stay close, Stranger, I'm going to let you ride in a few minutes."

Casey rode into the grove of trees and dismounted. She peered at the strap in the thickening shadows; then she began to tug at the flap of leather. Stranger nudged her leg and Casey stooped and patted the dog's head. "I'm glad you're here, Stranger," she said.

Casey tugged at the strap again, then swore as her fingernail tore into the quick.

"Damn! There isn't anything in the whole state of Texas built for a woman to handle!"

Stranger wiggled her bottom and looked toward Maude's back.

Casey stamped her foot and sucked on the injured finger. "Just wait till I'm ready, Stranger!" she said. She glared at the dog until the animal dropped to her stomach and put her chin on her forefeet.

"That's better," Casey said, and turned her attention back to the strap.

When Stranger growled, Casey stopped, stood still, and eased her hand toward the weapon on her hip. When her hand was close enough, she snatched at the pistol and twisted around as the dirt from Stranger's heels struck her ankles.

Casey waved the pistol at the man and let Stranger gnaw at his leg.

"Don't shoot! Don't shoot! Call off your dog, please, ma'am. I'm not here to hurt you!"

"Stranger! That's enough!"

Casey stared in astonishment as Stranger immediately stopped her attack and came and sat by her side.

"Where on earth did *you* come from?" Casey asked.

"I was sitting behind that big tree over there when you rode in. I thought maybe you would help me."

Casey looked at the dirt-covered city clothes, the dented derby, and the trouser leg Stranger had torn, and lowered the pistol.

"What happened to you?" she asked. "Before my dog began to eat your leg, I mean."

The little man snatched the battered hat from his head and brushed at his clothes with the other hand.

"Permit me to introduce myself," he said. "I am Gaylord M. Fontaine, most recently from DeKalb, Illinois. I represent the Glidden Fence Company of that city. I rented a horse in town and the fool thing threw me and ran away."

Casey slid her gun back into its holster and noted the

relieved look on the man's face. Then he stepped toward her suddenly and she clawed at the weapon again. She saw the spurt of dust between the man's feet, then heard the sound of the shot as her old problem with the hair trigger returned. "Stay where you are," she commanded.

Casey moved backward until she felt Maude's reassuring bulk behind her, and kept the pistol leveled until the little man clasped his hands and dropped to his knees.

"Please, lady! I wouldn't hurt you or anyone else! I'm a stranger in a strange place and I need help!" Casey waited while the man, still on his knees, backed away a few feet.

She felt Stranger nudge her leg. She glanced at the dog. Stranger's calm enough now, she thought. Casey put the gun away again.

"Well, mister, this isn't Illinois. One of the first things you need to learn is to not make sudden moves around people who are carrying guns. Now what is it you want me to do for you?"

"I, ah, guess I really don't know. I'm here a long way from town. I ache all over and now I've been dog bit and shot at and I really don't know what to do next."

Casey looked the man up and down again, held her breath, and thought for a moment.

"We're closer to my place than we are to town. Maybe you'd better come home with me. I'll feed you and you can sleep in the barn."

Casey turned back to Maude and set to work on the strap again. When the animal turned her head and rolled her eyes, Casey pushed against the horse's nose. "That's the way it is, Maude," she said. "You stay out of it."

Casey went to the other side of the horse and checked the stirrup for length. "No wonder it bothered me. One *was* longer than the other," she muttered.

"Beg pardon?"

"Just talking to myself," Casey said. He's no taller than I am, she thought. He can't see over Maude, either.

Casey moved back around the animal, put her foot in

the stirrup, and grasped the saddle horn. Then she pulled heself into the saddle and kicked her foot free of the sling. When she nodded to the man, he clambered up behind her.

While he settled, Casey pulled the gun to the space between her legs. She tugged until the heavy weapon lay comfortably against her body.

"What do I hold to?" he asked.

Casey watched Stranger pace as she waited for the signal that she could mount Maude.

"You can hold onto the dog," she said, and nodded to the animal.

As Stranger leaped, Casey leaned forward and made room for the dog between herself and the man. Maude danced sideways, Casey kicked her hard in the ribs, the horse settled, and Casey smiled as the man and the dog both tried to find a comfortable position.

Casey rode in silence until he spoke.

"Ma'am, why, ah—. Well, I was wondering why is it that the dog rides too?"

"I promised her," Casey answered over her shoulder, then turned her face forward and stared between Maude's ears at the narrow road ahead.

At home she stopped in the yard and waited for Stranger and Fontaine to dismount; then she climbed from the saddle.

"Take Maude to the barn, mister, unsaddle her, and give her some hay. I'll start supper."

Casey handed the reins to the man and stepped to one side for him to lead the animal away. She frowned as Fontaine didn't move but just stood and dug at the ground with his toe.

"Ma'am, I don't have any idea of how to do what you just asked me to do. I've never saddled or unsaddled a horse in my life. I . . . I'm sorry."

Casey snatched the leather strap from the man's hand.

"All right. I'll do it. Go in and see if you can start a fire in the stove without burning the house down. There's kindling in the wood box."

"I think I can do that," the man said.

Casey started for the barn with Maude; then she stopped and turned back.

"If you get the fire started, come out and sit on the porch where I can see you. I don't want any surprises when I walk through that door."

When Fontaine nodded his understanding, Casey led Maude to the barn. She pulled the saddle from the mare, slung it over the sawhorse, and unbuckled the throat latch of the bridle. Then she climbed the ladder to the loft and forked the hay down to Maude.

Strange person, she thought. I wonder whatever brought him to Texas?

As she closed the barn door, Casey glanced at the house and noted with satisfaction the smoke rising from the chimney. She looked quickly at the porch and frowned when she saw no sign of Fontaine. As she moved toward the house, she reached for her pistol. She lifted it an inch, then let it drop back in place. She hesitated for a moment, then spoke into the shadows, "Stranger, come stay close to me."

Casey felt the dog's nose bump her leg and she resumed her walk toward the house. When she reached the house, she flattened her back against the rough boards. She thought, where can he be? She worked her way carefully around the building to the back and peered through the window.

"Good Lord, Stranger! I believe he's stirring those beans. He's got supper nearly ready!"

She could feel Stranger's body wiggling in delight as she completed her circling of the house. Casey stepped onto the porch and went through the front door.

"I told you to wait on the porch," she said.

The little man turned and faced her.

"I'm sorry. I didn't mean to disturb you. I just wanted to be of some help."

Casey sighed and reached for the buckle to remove the gun belt, then hesitated. I believe I'll just shift it a little, she thought, and moved the belt to a more comfortable position.

"I have dinner nearly ready. If you'll have a seat, I'll serve you in a moment."

Casey poured water into the wash pan, glanced over her shoulder before turning her back, washed her hands, and then covered her face with soap and bent over to wash the suds away.

Pain from the strong soap struck her eyes and she groped for the towel. Suddenly Casey felt the rough cloth in her hand. Before she could see, she knew that Fontaine was only inches away. She stepped back quickly. "How'd you do that?" she asked.

"I was trained to do it."

"Trained? Trained to sneak up on people and hand them towels?"

"Among other things, yes. I was a domestic. My duty was to provide whatever my employer needed and to do it as quickly and quietly as possible."

Casey jerked her head toward the stove.

"Is that how you learned to cook?"

Casey hung the towel on its peg as the man nodded.

"Cooking was never my specialty but I can do a little of it."

Without thinking, Casey responded to Fontaine's gesture toward the table, carefully laid for one. She accepted the chair he held for her. When she was seated, she looked again at the table.

"You didn't set a place for yourself? Aren't you hungry?"

"I will if you wish."

Casey waited while he arranged a place for himself and served the food he had prepared. When he joined her at the table, she began to eat. When he did not speak, she broke the silence.

"You warmed up the biscuits."

"I found the food in the safe."

"What brings you to Texas, Mr. Fontaine?"

"I was tired of being a servant."

"You just quit the work you had been trained for and came to Texas?"

"Yes, in a way. I had heard there were opportunities in the West, so I left New York and made my way to Illinois before I ran out of money."

"Then what?"

"I was broke and hungry. I would have worked at anything. I would have even been willing to be a servant again."

"Well, did you?"

Fontaine rose and began to clear the table. He put the dish pan on the stove, filled it with water, and put the dishes in it.

"No, ma'am, I didn't. I didn't have to. I heard of a man named Glidden, who had invented something he wanted to sell. I went to see him and he hired me."

"You sell something, then?"

"Yes, Mr. Glidden tells me that if I will work hard I will make a great deal of money, but it hasn't happened yet.

Suddenly the sight of the little man washing dishes repulsed and angered Casey.

"I can't believe you came in here and prepared this food and are standing there washing the dishes. What kind of man are you, Mr. Fontaine?"

When she saw the shoulders square and the spine stiffen, Casey regretted her remark. Fontaine turned and faced her and the anger showed in his face.

"I can't believe that you carry a gun and fire it at people. That you pick up strangers on the road and that you let your dog ride on your horse. What kind of woman are you, Mrs. Lee?"

CHAPTER 10

"MR. Fontaine, I was wrong. I should have never said such a thing. I don't know what has gotten into me. You have done everything you could to be helpful. Please accept my apology."

Relief flooded Casey as Fontaine smiled.

"No, Mrs. Lee. It is I who should apologize. I am a guest here; I should have held my temper. I think we both have had a hard day."

Casey crossed the room and extended her hand and smiled. "Friends?" she asked. The strength of Fontaine's grip surprised her. "Friends," he said.

Casey moved the lamp closer and studied the short piece of twisted wire in her hand.

"You mean to tell me that this thin piece of wire can keep just about any kind of livestock under control?"

"It's the barbs that do it, ma'am. No animal will push against the wire once it's felt those sharp points."

"That makes sense to me. Why won't the storekeepers buy it?"

The little man sighed and Casey waited for him to speak. I really feel sorry for him, she thought. I haven't felt sorry for anyone but myself for a long time. Then she realized the man was speaking again.

"Most of the merchants seem to be afraid to carry the wire. They say they will lose customers if they do. Some say it will injure the stock but mostly I think they are afraid of the big ranchers. Then, too, some just don't believe that it is strong enough to hold livestock."

Casey leaned forward in her chair.

"The big ranchers? Why would they care?"

"They don't want to see all this free open range fenced off."

Casey pushed the wire toward Fontaine.

"You'll probably have to get someone to sell it who doesn't have anything else to sell. Then they wouldn't have to be afraid."

While she waited for Fontaine to speak, Casey felt the strong push of Stranger's nose against her leg and she reached for a biscuit on the plate. Without looking she dropped the biscuit toward the floor and waited for the sound of the animal's mouth to close over the biscuit in midair.

"Stranger's little treat," she said. "She's learned to expect it at every meal."

"You seem to be very fond of the animal."

Casey paused a moment and cocked her head, thinking. Then she patted the red head.

"This dog is a definite burden to me at times. But then, she is company too, so I guess I spoil her some."

Fontaine put the polished piece of wire into its little leather case.

"You run this place alone, then?"

"There's not much to run. My husband had great hopes for it before he was killed but he had only gotten started. I'll probably have to sell the farm and move to town. I bought the livery stable just today."

Fontaine tugged at his tie, then looked across the table. "May I?"

Casey nodded. "I wonder why I feel comfortable with him?" she asked herself. "Maybe it's because he is so small," she mused.

"Was it your horse that threw me, then, Mrs. Lee?"

Casey brought herself back to the conversation with a start.

"No, oh no! I didn't buy the horses. Just the stable."

Fontaine slipped the little case into his coat pocket.

"May I ask what you plan to do with the stable?"

"I have a plan, Mr. Fontaine."

Casey rose and paced the floor as she spoke.

"The barn is large and I plan to make a place in one corner where I can live if I want to."

Fontaine nodded. "Then you wouldn't have to stay out here alone. That makes sense."

"That's not all," Casey said. "I intend to change the rest of the place, too. I am going to make a place where the women around here can bring whatever they have that they might want to sell. I will provide a place for them to sell their wares. Eggs or quilts or whatever. Women never seem to have a way to get their hands on any cash, so I know this just has to work. I'll take a percentage and everything will work out fine for . . ."

Casey stopped in her tracks as a faint smile began to play around Fontaine's lips.

"You find my plan amusing, Mr. Fontaine?"

"No, ma'am, it's not amusing at all. It's just that, well, it's not really a plan. It is some thoughts that you had that might work and, then again, they might not."

Casey bit her lip and waited.

"Even if it works the way you want it to, there is very little money to be made from it."

"Why do you say that?"

"You said it yourself. The things that these women have to sell will be things that women buy. Their husbands have some cash but the women do not. Poof! There goes your business."

Casey sank into a chair as the tears began to well in her eyes.

"I've wasted my money, then," she said.

Fontaine put his elbows on the table and looked at her over his clasped hands. "Maybe not."

Stranger's sudden bark startled Casey and she looked quickly at Fontaine. She saw him glance at the dog, then toward the door. Then she heard the sound of the horse in the yard.

"Hello in the house! Hello! Anybody home?"

"Why that sounds like . . . I believe that's Red McCaslin," Casey said aloud.

She picked up the lamp and held it high to shed as much light as possible as she stepped onto the porch.

"Yes, Mr. McCaslin, I'm here. What's the trouble?"

She waited while the man worked the huge horse as close to the porch as possible and leaned in the saddle.

"Buck said he rented a horse to a drummer today and the horse come back without him. He asked me to ride out this way and see if I could find the fellow. Thought he might be hurt or something."

Casey turned at the sound of Fontaine's voice from the doorway behind her.

"I'm fine. This lady has been kind enough to take me in."

Casey stepped to one side and shifted the lamp to her left hand as Fontaine came onto the porch. She waited as he stepped from the porch to the ground. He looks almost like a child standing beside that big horse, she thought.

"Mr. McCaslin, this is Mr. Fontaine," she said.

"Well, little man, I'm glad to see you're all right. You just climb up here behind me and I'll take you back to town."

Casey lowered the lamp as Fontaine stood silent for a moment before he spoke, and she could tell the man was offended and puzzled.

"Mr. McCaslin, I appreciate your interest in my welfare and your offer to help. But this lady has offered to let me sleep in her barn tonight and we were in the middle of a discussion. I believe I will stay here and finish that."

"Get on this horse, mister!"

Casey jumped at the cold sound of McCaslin's voice. She set the lamp on the porch floor and waited to see what Fontaine would do.

"I believe I will stay here, sir," Fontaine said.

The glow of the lamp shone only on the horse's legs as he began to dance in the yard, and Casey knew that McCaslin had tightened his grip on the reins.

"I'm going to tell you one more time, little man. Get on this horse!"

Casey dropped her hand to her gun butt and waited while McCaslin worked his horse close to the porch again and leaned in the saddle to speak to her.

"Casey, you ought to have sense enough to know that I'm not going to let another man stay out here all night with my woman."

Rage blinded Casey and the gun felt good as it filled her hand and she heard her voice in a high-pitched scream. It almost sounded as though it belonged to someone else.

She shouted, "Red McCaslin, if you're not off my place in one minute, I'm going to blow you out of that saddle!"

Fontaine scrambled away as the horse reared. The little man was on the porch beside Casey by the time the animal's front hoofs hit the ground. Casey kept the gun pointed at the darkness and screamed again at the figure receding in the darkness.

"Damn you to hell, Red McCaslin! I'm nobody's woman!"

"Good heavens! Who was he?" Fontaine asked in a conversational tone.

"I'm not really sure," Casey said.

She could feel the uneasiness in Fontaine as he spoke again.

"I don't mean to pry but you seemed to know each other rather well. He called you his woman."

"He said it but I'm not," Casey growled.

Casey turned on her heel, stomped into the house, threw herself into the chair, and put her head on her arms.

"I should have shot him," she sobbed.

She felt Stranger's nose nudge her leg; then she heard Fontaine quietly seat himself at the table with her. When Fontaine cleared his throat, Casey raised her head.

"Would you like for me to leave now, Mrs. Lee? I don't want to cause you problems."

Casey gave her full attention to the man again. Lord, I wish he would leave, she thought; then she spoke sharply: "Of course not! Where on earth would you go in the middle of the night?"

"I really don't know. The very thought frightens me. I could have gone with that man but I could not bring myself to let him order me out of here."

Casey studied Fontaine for a moment. He really is terrified. She stood and walked to the bedroom door. "You'll sleep in here tonight," she said. Then she walked into the room and lit the lamp on the bedside table. She returned to the kitchen and looked at Fontaine coldly.

"I'll be in later," she said.

When Fontaine opened his mouth to speak, she raised her hand.

"If you touch me during the night, I'll blow your brains out."

As Fontaine nodded and moved quietly through the bedroom door, Casey seated herself at the table again. She sat and thought and cursed the mixed feelings she always had when Red McCaslin was around.

Then she stood, blew out the lamp, and made her way through the darkness to her bedroom.

CHAPTER 11

CASEY stood in the darkness and listened for a moment to the heavy breathing. She took the gun from its holster and carefully placed it on the floor beside the bed. She unbuckled the gun belt and let it silently slide to the floor beside the weapon. She stood on one foot and tugged until a boot came off, then stood on the other foot and removed the second boot. As quietly as possible, she lay down beside Fontaine.

"I must be insane," she murmured into the darkness.

Then she shifted herself as close as possible to the edge of the bed, closed her eyes, and waited for sleep.

The dream, when it came, was strange and troubled and laced with the sound of a sobbing child. Casey opened her eyes, stared into the darkness, and tried to locate the sound. Then she remembered Fontaine in the bed beside her and realized that the sound came from him.

She propped herself on one elbow and looked at him. She hesitated a moment; then she sighed, moved herself closer to the little man, and drew him to her. Casey put his head on her breast and stroked and patted him like a child until the sobbing became a whimper.

After a while Casey slipped her aching arm from under Fontaine's head and rolled silently from the bed. She felt for her boots and carried them out of the bedroom into the dark kitchen. She sat in a chair and tugged on the boots. When they were in place, she tiptoed across the room to the wash pan and reached toward the water bucket for the dipper. It was empty. With a sigh, she felt for the bail, picked up the bucket, and went out the front door.

Casey crossed the yard in the predawn darkness and set the bucket on the rough boards of the well housing. She unwound the rope and let the other bucket descend; it reached the water and she waited while it began to fill. Then she listened to the tiny squeak of the pulley as she tugged on the rope.

I wonder if all well pulleys squeak, she thought, and pulled harder on the rope.

First she saw the flare of the match on the other side of the well housing; then she heard the sound of the voice and smelled the cigarette smoke.

"I'll have to kill him now, you know."

The well rope burned as it ran through her hands. She heard the bucket hit the sides of the well on its way down, then heard the thug sound as the bucket hit the water, and she jumped back from the well and reached for her hip.

Even as she reached, she knew the gun wasn't there. She could see it clearly in her mind where she had left it lying beside the bed.

Rage flooded Casey at the sight of Red McCaslin as his dim form rose from the other side of the well.

"What are you doing here?" she demanded. "I told you to leave last night!"

Casey waited for the man to speak, and the longer she waited, the more rage overwhelmed her.

"Who the hell do you think you are anyway? You can't come out here and start this kind of thing with me. I hardly know you!"

"That's not my fault. I've done everything I could think of to get your attention."

I'd feel better if there were more light out here, Casey thought.

She waited and said nothing while McCaslin fumbled in his shirt pocket, pulled out the sack of tobacco, and deliberately rolled another cigarette. The silence grew and Casey tried desperately to think of something more to say. When McCaslin had lit the cigarette, he pulled the smoke into his lungs and propped his boot on the well.

"Well, Casey, I'm going to tell you about me. Then I'm going into that house and throw that runt out in the yard and shoot holes in him."

Her mother's words rang again in Casey's mind:

"Casey, if a gentleman wishes to talk about himself, sometimes it is best to listen carefully no matter how bored you may be . . ."

In spite of her mother's words, the rage remained and Casey snapped out the words without thinking: "I already know all about you that I need to know. Texas is full of men like you. They talk slow, shoot fast, and have no visible means of support!"

McCaslin's sudden laughter came as a shock and Casey took a step backward and said nothing.

"You really don't know anything at all about me, do you?"

Casey shook her head.

"I thought . . . well I hoped that Mrs. Rogers might have told you something about me."

Casey shook head again. In the growing light, she could see that the man rolled the cigarette butt between his thumb and forefinger until the fire was out before he dropped it on the ground.

"I work for the Cattlemen's Association," he said. "My job is to be in the right place at the right time, and when I get there, to be fast with my gun. It's usually enough to protect the herds. If anything really bad happens, it's part of my job to back that fat man in town that wears the star."

Casey moved closer and looked at his hands in the growing light. They're shaped like William's, she thought. Except for the red curly hair on his fingers.

"If you are such a responsible person, why are you out here acting like this?" she demanded.

"Mrs. Lee, please believe me. I mean well. I haven't been completely responsible since the day you slammed into me on the sidewalk in town. I have wanted you from that very minute on. I can't seem to think of anything else."

Casey listened carefully and could feel the control of the situation slipping into her hands.

"Mr. McCaslin, you certainly have not made a good impression on me. If you are as interested as you say, you'll get on that horse and ride to town. You talk to Mrs. Rogers. If she is willing to formally introduce us, I will consider letting you call on me."

The first rays of the morning sun struck McCaslin's face and Casey could see him clearly now. She saw him reach for his hat and tip it over his eyes to screen out the sun. Then she saw him freeze in position, his hands still on the brim of his hat. Why on earth is he doing that? she thought. Then she saw the small hand reach from behind and close over the handle of the big gun that rode McCaslin's hip.

"Don't move, McCaslin," Casey said. "That will be Mr. Fontaine with my thirty-eight. It has a hair trigger."

"I know about the hair trigger. The gunsmith told me."

Casey took a deep breath and spoke as calmly as she could.

"Mr. Fontaine, that *is* you behind Mr. McCaslin, is it not?"

Casey strained to hear the faint answer.

"Yes, it's me."

"Mr. Fontaine, that weapon you are holding fires very easily. Now I do not want you to shoot Mr. McCaslin even accidentally. So I want you to very carefully take your finger off the trigger."

Casey waited and watched McCaslin's face, then glanced quickly at his arms while watching for any sign of movement.

"Have you done that, Mr. Fontaine?"

Casey felt the heartbeat in her eardrums while she waited for the small voice.

"I'm afraid to. He'll do something."

That thing is going to go off any minute, Casey thought.

"That's all right, Mr. Fontaine. Just bring Mr. McCaslin's weapon to me."

Casey waited again.

"I can't."

My God, he's so scared, he's frozen in his tracks.

"Why not, Mr. Fontaine?"

"I, well, ah, I'm not dressed. I'm in my underwear. I can't come out from behind McCaslin."

Casey could see the beads on McCaslin's brow and she knew the man understood the danger he was in.

"Have you removed your finger from the trigger of my weapon?"

"Yes, ma'am. I have his gun pointed at him now."

Casey looked quickly at McCaslin but the relief she expected did not show in his face. She nodded at McCaslin.

"Hair trigger, huh?"

She held her breath again as McCaslin slowly nodded.

"Mr. Fontaine, if I close my eyes, will you bring me Mr. McCaslin's weapon?"

"If you keep them closed."

Casey squeezed her eyes tight.

"My eyes are closed, Mr. Fontaine. I want you to bring me Mr. McCaslin's gun; then I want you to run as fast as you can to the house. I won't look till you are inside."

Casey stood with her eyes closed and her hands outstretched. When she felt the hardness of the weapon in her hand, she opened her eyes and looked at McCaslin as he lowered his arms. From the corner of her eye, she could see Fontaine running for the house in his underwear.

Casey flipped the catch on the side of McCaslin's gun and let the cylinder fall. She emptied the cartridges on the ground and extended the weapon, butt first, to the big man. Then she nodded toward the house.

"That's the man you were going to kill for spending the night with me? she asked.

She waited for McCaslin to answer but he simply put the empty gun in his holster and looked at her.

Casey raised one eyebrow and smiled.

"Go talk to Mrs. Rogers," she said, then turned and walked toward the house.

CHAPTER 12

CASEY sat on the bench in front of her barn and watched the dust devil form at one end of the deserted street. It traveled with growing importance to the other end of town, then disappeared.

"That's me," she muttered. "That's me right there. That's all I do. I storm around, raise a little dust, then poof! Here I sit, wondering what to do next." She sighed and felt in her pocket for the crumpled letter. She smoothed it on her knee and read it again.

Dear Mrs. Lee:

I take my pen in hand to thank you for your recent kindness and hospitality. Things have been a little better for me since I left your town.

I have managed to sell some of the wire and Mr. Glidden writes that he is pleased to see that I am making some progress. He says, however, that something must be done to develop the business in your area.

I have made a bold move. I have taken the liberty of shipping you one thousand rolls of Glidden wire. I am sure that if you will store it in your barn, that you can eventually sell it at a nice profit.

The wire is cosigned to you at one dollar per roll and all you have to do is to sell it for two dollars per roll to make a thousand dollars on this first shipment.

Mr. Glidden assures me that if we can get substantial amounts of wire located in strategic points in Texas, that it will begin to sell faster.

I realize that this is a presumptuous move on my part. I had to explain to Mr. Glidden why I was sure that you would pay for the wire once it had been sold.

I told him how you had kept your promise to your dog, Stranger, to let her ride on the horse. That was the day you found me in the grove. Mr. Glidden just looked thoughtful and said, "Ship the wire."

I hope you will forgive me for shipping first without your approval but I had no time to get your permission.

Sincerely,
Gaylord Fontaine

P.S. I have at last gathered the courage to tell you that the night I spent in your home was the most beautiful experience of my entire life.

Casey stuffed the letter back in her pocket, rose, looked both ways down the street, and then started toward Rogers's store. She glanced down at the dog beside her.

"Stranger, I'm only going to the store. Do you have to follow me everywhere?"

She felt the familiar nudge against her leg and relented.

"Well, come on, then."

At the door of the store, Casey held her hand palm out toward Stranger and said, "Stay!" Then she waited while the dog settled herself on the sidewalk.

At the sound of the little bell on the door, Mrs. Rogers turned and faced Casey.

"Good morning, Casey. Did you get settled in all right?"

"Yes, I guess you'd have to say I'm settled. The men Buck got together to move me handled things a little more roughly than I thought they would. They broke a leg off the stove but I put a rock under it and it seems to be all right."

"That's men for you. They never seem to think about those things. Every time Mr. Rogers and I have moved, something has gotten broken. I would never have been able to save the tea set if I hadn't wrapped it in a quilt and carried it on my lap."

Casey nodded and wondered if Mrs. Rogers could tell her anything about what to do with a thousand rolls of barbed wire.

"Speaking of tea, Casey, would you like some? We'll have to drink it out here. I'm alone again today."

"Where is Mr. Rogers?"

"He's down the street at the harness shop . . . he says. If he's where I think he is, he won't be back till night. He starts earlier in the day now."

Casey nodded. "I'd love some tea."

She leaned on the counter and waited while the older woman went through the burlap curtain to the back room.

Mrs. Rogers returned with the tea and pushed Casey's cup across the counter to her. Casey leaned over her side of the counter, sipped the hot liquid, and opened her mouth to speak when the other woman spoke first.

"Casey, how are you getting along with Red McCaslin?"

Casey hesitated. "Better than I really want to," she said. "He tries to stop by every day that he is in town. I really don't quite know whtat to do with him. Actually I think I am a little afraid of him."

When Mrs. Rogers straightened herself suddenly and squinted her eyes, Casey wished she hadn't spoken.

"Casey, has he done something? I felt sure he was a respectable man or I would never have done that introduction thing he insisted on."

"It's not that, Mrs. Rogers. It's, well, I don't like him much but when he's around I get these feelings."

As Mrs. Rogers's face relaxed and Casey began to see the beginning of a smile, she suddenly felt defensive.

"Well, after all, Mrs. Rogers, no one knows how many men he's killed."

"Well, I'm pretty sure he has no intention of killing you, Casey."

Casey saw the woman's quick glance at her .38.

"Unless you draw on him first and he moves before he has time to think."

"It's not that, Mrs. Rogers. It's well, I don't like him much but when he's around I get these feelings."

"You and most of the rest of the women in this county. Women are like that with dangerous men."

Casey felt the color in her face as she spoke.

"Well, I don't like it."

Mrs. Rogers put her empty cup on the counter and frowned.

"Casey, has anybody said anything to you about your buying that livery stable?"

"Heavens no, Mrs. Rogers. What could anyone have to say about that?"

Casey waited while the older woman filled the cups again and seemed to think for a moment before she answered.

"Nobody would I suppose except . . . except maybe Anthony."

Casey sipped at the tea.

"Anthony? Anthony. William introduced me to a Mr. Anthony when we first got here. Said he was a big rancher. He seemed to be a nice man."

Casey frowned and studied Mrs. Rogers's face. The woman seemed to hesitate before she spoke again.

"Anthony is not a nice man, Casey. Nearly everyone here is afraid of him."

"Why?" Casey asked. "Why would people be afraid of him?"

Casey steadied her hand as she put her cup back on the counter and she wished Mrs. Rogers would talk about something else.

"He's a greedy man, Casey, and he wants to run everything around here. He keeps a rough bunch around him, especially that Willie. The one they call the widow maker. Anthony has managed to take almost complete control of the Cattlemen's Association and there are quite a few folks who wouldn't think of selling property without offering it to him first."

Casey stood silently before the large woman. I don't want to know all this, she thought. Why does she insist on telling me? I suppose I'd better say something, though.

"I never heard of such a thing, Mrs. Rogers. Why would anyone do that?"

Casey grew uneasy as Mrs. Rogers's patience began to wear thin.

"Because, Casey . . ."

She's talking to me as though I were a child, Casey thought. I'd better pay attention to this.

"Sometimes people who don't do things Anthony's way have trouble. He's a powerful man. Mr. Rogers said he quarreled with Buck last night in the saloon because Buck sold you that barn. He's always wanted your place. He was trying to buy it from Bill Black's widow before your William came to town."

When the little bell on the front door tinkled, Casey reached for a catalogue on the counter. She flipped the pages, hoping to see something about barbed wire, and then decided to leave.

Outside the store, Stranger sniffed her leg and then rose and trotted beside Casey down the street. Before she reached the barn, she could see a small boy playing. He put one foot on the bench, then stood on one foot till his other foot reached the level of the bench. Then he pushed with both feet and jumped backward till he landed in the dust on both feet. He would make a mark in the dust, then try again for a longer jump.

Casey waited for him to make his last jump before she spoke.

"Don't hurt yourself."

The boy stopped and stared at her.

"You Miz Casey Lee?"

"Yes, I am. Who are you?"

"I'm the Jones boy. We live west of here. My pa works for Mr. Grimley sometimes."

"Well, hello, Mr. Jones. What can I do for you?"

Casey tried not to smile while the boy straightened his shoulders and looked directly at her.

"Mr. Red McCaslin et supper at our place last night."

"Yes?"

"When Pa told him we was coming to town today, Mr. McCaslin gave me a dime."

"That was nice."

"He said I wasn't to spend it till I found you and told you something. He told me to tell you he would be back in town tonight and he would come to see you if it was all right."

"Well, thank you, Mr. Jones."

Casey reached to pat the boy on the head but drew her hand back as the boy moved his head quickly to one side, turned, and ran toward Rogers's store.

Casey slowly walked the length of her barn and wished she could fight all the thoughts from her mind.

I wonder how many of these stalls a thousand rolls of wire will fill? I wonder when the wire will arrive. Where could McCaslin have gone this time? Can I really sell the wire? Mr. Rogers refused to buy it. Mrs. Rogers says he was wrong. Is all the hair on his body red and curly? The boy didn't say what time.

CHAPTER 13

CASEY turned up the flame of the lamp and peered into the mirror. She smoothed her dark hair with her brush and studied the reflection again.

"Well, Stranger, I've looked better but this will just have to do. I wonder what's keeping McCaslin?"

Casey seated herself in the rocking chair and listened to the sounds her barn made in the beginning wind. She watched the flicker of the lamplight on the wall. I should have trimmed that wick, she thought. The boy didn't say he would be late. Then, "Stranger come away from that window. You're a bigger fool than I am. He probably isn't coming at all."

Casey rose, went to the door, stepped into the darkness, and looked each way down the street.

"The only lights are from the saloon," she murmured, and eased herself onto the wooden bench. She sat in the dark, stroked Stranger's head, and recalled her mother's words: "Casey, one receives only in the parlor . . ."

My place is big enough, she thought, but having everything in one room is bad. Every time he is here I see him looking at that bed.

Casey rose quietly from the bench as a strong gust of wind blew dust into her eyes. The barn creaked louder than before. Suddenly the dust, the wind, the creaking of the barn, and Maude's uneasy pounding at her stall were more than Casey could stand. She started for the door.

"He's not coming, Stranger. We're stupid to sit out here and wait for the man."

Inside, Casey blew out the lamp and undressed in the darkness. She reached for the cotton gown, held it to her breast, and stood listening to the rising wind and to the barn complaining in the night. Then she dropped the gown to the floor and slid beneath the one light cover on the bed. She lay and enjoyed the feel of the light blanket against her body and tried not to think of Red McCaslin.

"He probably won't live much longer, anyway," she murmured. "At his age, he is bound to be slowing down some. Somebody will get him someday soon."

Then in the back of her mind she let the thought begin that had nudged her again and again for the past two hours.

Maybe someone has. Maybe somebody got behind him someplace tonight!

Casey didn't try to suppress her feeling of panic. Instead she forced her mind to focus on clearly formed pictures of how it could have been. Around a campfire, in a saloon someplace, anyplace. The slow drawling words, the sudden decision, the flash of gunfire. Then the aftermath. The time of backing away, then the sudden departure of the winner.

Casey tried to torture herself with the thought of a fallen Red McCaslin but the little story that she built in her mind would not have it that way. Each time she could see only a virtuous and victorious Red McCaslin.

She heard Stranger's low growl first, then the sound of the wagon in the hallway of the barn. Casey rolled from the bed, dipped water into the wash pan, and dashed it on her face. She threw on her clothes, strapped on the .38, and stepped into the early morning light with Stranger at her side.

She stood speechless, staring at the four wagons, one

behind the other, strung the length of her barn. She watched as one of the men approached her, fumbling in his pocket.

Casey waited while the man found a paper and unfolded it. "Miss Casey Lee?" he asked.

Casey nodded.

"My name is Dobson. Where did you want us to put your wire?"

"I, ah, well, I'm not quite sure. Let me see . . ."

"Our deal was to deliver and stack the wire wherever you said. We're not to stack it higher than a man can reach comfortable."

Casey pointed to the stalls in the barn across from Maude's.

"Do you think those three stalls will hold it all?"

Casey waited while Dobson slowly turned and surveyed the stalls. "We'll see," he said, and turned and walked back to the wagons.

At Stranger's nudge, Casey turned and went back to her living quarters.

"We'll eat soon, Stranger. Right now we have to attend to business."

Casey brushed her hair and listened to the sound of the men unloading the wire. I wonder why that sound makes me feel a little proud and a little afraid at the same time? she asked herself. Then she spoke aloud to Stranger: "Well, we're in the wire business now. I can see that it will make money if I can just sell the stuff."

Casey prepared her breakfast and then fed Stranger as the sound of Buck's anvil began. Then she went back into the barn to check the progress of the men.

The small group of men standing in the doorway of her barn startled her so that Casey gasped but then spoke as she recognized some of them.

"Good morning, Mr. Anthony, Mr. Buckmaster, everybody. I'm getting into the wire business. I hope you will all be good customers."

Casey didn't move when the large man, Anthony, stepped forward.

"Mrs. Lee, does Red McCaslin know about this?"

She felt her anger begin to rise.

"Mr. Anthony, Mr. McCaslin calls upon me from time to time but I have never felt a need to discuss my business affairs with him."

Casey watched in amazement as the man touched the brim of his hat. "I thought not," he said, then turned and walked away.

"I feel as though I've been slapped," she murmured as the others followed Anthony to Buck's blacksmith shop. Then she turned and went into the barn.

"Well, Stranger, that Mr. Anthony isn't very impressive for a big cattleman."

Inside the barn Dobson came toward her with a large metal sign in his hands. He leaned the sign against the wall as he spoke.

"Here's your sign. I put the stretcher in the first stall of wire over there."

"Stretcher? Stretcher? Oh, the stretcher. Well, yes, that's fine."

She idly watched the man while he opened his mouth, then closed it and turned away. I wonder what a stretcher is? she thought, then turned her attention to the man again as he faced her.

"Mrs. Lee, you don't know anything at all about barbed wire, do you?"

"I know enough . . ." Casey stopped short and sighed.

"No, sir. I really don't know anything at all about it."

Casey leaned against the wall while the man took off his hat, wiped his brow, and seemed to think about the matter.

"Well, ma'am, wire is new and some folks don't like it much. I like it because it is the most practical thing that has come along in a long time."

"Mr. Fontaine told me that too," Casey said.

The man carefully creased his hat and put it back on his head.

"I've been hauling on contract for the Glidden Fence Company for some time and I've learned a little about the wire."

Casey shifted her weight.

"Could you give me some good advice? About selling the wire, I mean."

Casey watched, fascinated, while the man took off his hat, creased it again, and then turned it in his hands.

"Well, ma'am, the main thing that I have learned is that when I haul the first load into a town, there is always somebody that gets real wrought up about it. There are some places that I go back to with more loads and there are some places that I never go back to."

Casey tried to ignore the weakness in her knees as she moved toward the bench.

"I can handle myself," she said.

"Yes, ma'am, I expect you can. I noticed your weapon. But that thing is not going to help you sell wire. Let me tell you a little about it. Then if you ever sell any, you can tell the customer how it should be put up."

Casey made room on the bench and motioned the man to sit beside her.

When he was beside her, the man hung his hat between his legs and twirled it slowly in his fingers.

"The way I see it, if a man puts the wire up the right way, he will like what it does for him and he may buy more. But if he puts it up wrong, he won't like it and probably will never come back for more."

Casey listened and tried to remember while the man scratched diagrams in the dirt. I hope I remember some of this, she thought.

Dobson carefully drew his diagrams in the dirt while Casey looked on.

"I guess the most important part is the corner posts," he said.

"Are they different from the others?"

"Yes, they need to be heavier and stronger than the line posts, if possible, and they should always be braced."

"I'll never understand," Casey told herself. "I hope he can make it clear to me."

"Why are the corner posts so important?" she asked.

"Strain. The corner posts get more strain than the line posts."

Casey shook her head.

"Why?"

Dobson looked up at her then. "He's disgusted with me," Casey told herself. "I hope he doesn't just give up on me."

"You do understand that this wire needs to be stretched tight, don't you?"

Casey wrinkled and smiled at Dobson the way William had liked.

"I suppose that might help some," she said.

Dobson rose and stood before her for a moment. I've done it, Casey thought. He's going to give up on me and I'll never learn about this stuff. Dobson moved toward her and she made room for him on the bench.

"Let's start over at the beginning," he said.

Casey nodded.

"Please do. I need to know this. I know I do. If you'll just be patient, I'll try to understand."

Dobson looked at her again, took a deep breath, and let it out. He looks at me as though I were a backward child, Casey thought.

Dobson began again.

"First of all the wire needs to be stretched pretty tight or it is not of much use at all. That's where it gets its strength."

Casey nodded.

"I can see that."

"If we stretch the wire, that puts a strain someplace, doesn't it?"

"Go on," Casey said. "I think I'm beginning to understand."

"To stretch this wire, we have to fasten it to something strong so that it will accept the strain. So we take a strong corner post, then we brace that post with another post that runs at an angle from the top of the corner post to the ground like this."

In the dirt Dobson drew a diagram of a braced corner post.

"Then we know that since this is a corner post that we will have wire running in another direction, probably at a right angle, so the post needs to be able to accept that strain also."

"Why not put another brace running in that direction too?" Casey asked.

When Dobson smiled and nodded, Casey relaxed a little.

"Exactly," Dobson said. "So now we have a strong corner post braced in two directions."

Casey felt a sense of excitement begin to build within.

"So what do we do next?" she asked.

"Well, let's assume that we have our braced corner post and that we have set our line posts in each direction."

"What's a line post?" Casey asked, then wished she had waited to see if he would explain without a question from her.

"Line posts are simply smaller posts that hold the wire, and while they need to be well set in the ground, they do not accept the double strain that the corner post does, so they usually need no bracing."

Casey frowned and tried to create a mental image of their fence up to this point. When her mind saw the braced corner post and a long line of line posts, she nodded again.

"How do we get the wire on the posts?" she asked.

"We're back to the corner posts again," Dobson said. "First you take a good strong wrap around the corner post and staple the wire to that."

Casey squinted her eyes and tried to visualize the "wrap" around the corner post.

"Top or bottom?" she asked.

"I usually start at the bottom. No special reason, I just think it makes sense to build something from the bottom up."

Casey let a feel of confidence flow through herself now

that she could see in her mind's eye all that Dobson had told her.

"Now that we have that strong wrap we can string the wire."

"String the wire?"

"Yes. The wire is unrolled and laid on the ground next to the line posts."

"On the ground?"

"Yes, now we are ready for the next step, stretching the wire."

"I know what's next," Casey said. "The stretcher."

"Not necessarily," he said. "Though, if it were a short fence, you would be right."

"Let's decide it's a short fence, so you can tell me how to use the stretcher."

When Dobson smiled and nodded, Casey settled herself to listen about the stretcher. He's such a patient man, she thought, and so kind to go to all this trouble with me. I'll bet he wouldn't hurt a fly.

"The stretcher is really just a small block and tackle," Dobson said.

"Block and tackle? What's a block and tackle?"

When Dobson paused and seemed lost in thought for a moment, Casey could see that he was struggling to form an answer to her question and she wished that she hadn't asked.

"Mrs. Lee, a block and tackle is a device used to lift weights and to exert large forces. It is made of ropes and pulleys. The pulleys are mounted . . ."

"I haven't the slightest idea of what he is talking about," Casey told herself, and tried to concentrate harder.

"I'll just show you the stretcher and show you how it works," Dobson was saying. "You just attach one set of pulleys to something strong, and the other pulley is fitted with a clamp that will seize onto the wire between the barbs, and this way the wire can be stretched tight."

Casey could feel the relief in the man when she nodded, and she was almost afraid to ask her next question.

"Mr. Dobson, you said the stretcher was for stretching a short fence. What about a long one?"

"You hitch a horse to it."

"You what?"

Dobson smiled.

You just make your wrap around the corner post, then string out the long strand of wire next to the line posts and hitch a horse to the end of it and have the animal pull. The animal holds the wire in place while someone fastens the wire to the line posts. The whole thing is much simpler to do than it seems when we talk about it."

Casey studied the diagrams a little longer, then straightened herself and rubbed the small of her back.

"Well, Mr. Dobson, I haven't been in the wire business over two hours and my back hurts already."

As she straightened herself, Casey glanced toward the blacksmith shop and for a moment her eyes locked with Anthony's.

"I wonder why he just stands there with his arms crossed and stares at us," she murmured.

CHAPTER 14

CASEY returned Anthony's stare for a moment, then spun on her heel and walked into her barn. She watched while the men unloaded the last roll of wire and put it into place. When Dobson handed her the freight bill, she read it and then held it out to him.

"What should I do with this, Mr. Dobson?"

"It's my release. When you sign it, that's proof that I delivered the wire, the staples, and the rest of the equipment."

Casey looked to the right and to the left for a flat surface smooth enough to write on. She moved to the long flat box on top of the stack of wire. She smoothed the paper over the stenciled letters *Dixie Stretcher* and started her signature.

"You didn't count the wire, ma'am."

Casey looked over her shoulder at the man, holding his hat in his hand.

"Oh, I'm sure that's not necessary. If you say it's all there . . ."

"I don't say it's all there. I counted the wire when it was loaded but we've been on the road for several days and I don't stay awake day and night to guard these loads."

Casey wished her heart wouldn't beat faster at such a simple thing.

"You think some of it is missing, then?"

Casey peered at the man and tried to understand, while

Dobson put his hat on and pushed it to the back of his head.

"No, I didn't say that, either. What I'm trying to do is teach you how to check in a shipment."

I'd better listen, Casey thought, while the man walked to one of the stacks of wire and put his hand on it.

"This wire was sent to you on consignment. That means that you agreed to pay for it when it is sold."

Casey nodded and waited for Dobson to continue.

"So, naturally, when the time comes to settle up, you owe for every roll of the wire that isn't here. If you didn't receive any part of the shipment, you still owe for it and you would not only lose the cost of the wire, but you would lose the profit that could have been made also."

Casey nodded again.

"I think I understand, but tell me, wouldn't I make the money back when I sold some more of the wire?"

When Dobson sighed, crossed his arms, and leaned against the wall, Casey felt her pulse begin to pound again. He's disgusted with me now, she thought. I hope he doesn't just leave or something before he explains.

"Am I wrong, Mr. Dobson?"

"When you lose money, you can't ever make it *back*."

"Why? I would have thought . . ."

"Ma'am, it's not my place to tell you how to run your business. I'm sorry I spoke about it."

Casey put her hand on the man's arm.

"Please, Mr. Dobson. You said it yourself. I don't know the first thing about what I'm doing here."

Dobson shifted his weight and Casey removed her hand from his arm. I hope he isn't going to leave, she thought.

"Look at it this way, ma'am. If you make some money, that is something that you either brought about or else it just happened to you. You can see that, can't you?"

"Yes."

"Very well. The fact that you made that money has nothing to do with the fact that you took a loss sometime in the past."

Casey nodded. "I can see that, too," she said.

"So when you make money, you haven't made it back. You have simply made money. If you can do that, you can do it whether or not you have had the loss in the first place. So you haven't recovered the loss at all. The loss still stands and remains forever as a loss in your business career."

Casey extended her hand and waited for the man to take it in his.

"Mr. Dobson, I want to thank you for all you have done for me."

She held his hand in hers for a moment and enjoyed the feel of his callused palm. It's like William's, she thought. She withdrew her hand.

"Let's count the wire, Mr. Dobson."

Casey moved down the rows of wire while Dobson followed with his hat in his hands.

"You said the wire is stacked five high and three deep?"

"Yes, ma'am."

"I count nine hundred and ninety-five. That's five short."

She turned and faced Dobson's smile.

"You knew that all the time, didn't you?" Casey asked.

Casey waited while Dobson dug in his shirt pocket and came out with some crumpled bills and the freight bill and handed them all to her.

"I sold the five rolls to a woman who said she wanted to fence her garden. I didn't think you'd mind. That's the money for it. If you will sign my freight bill, I'll be leaving now."

Casey signed the freight bill and then counted the money.

"Ten dollars! That means I've made five dollars already, doesn't it?"

When Dobson smiled again, Casey let a happy feeling slip into place.

"Oh, Mr. Dobson! You've helped me so much. How can I ever repay you?"

"Coffee."

"Coffee? Coffee. Of course, come on up to my quarters."

In her quarters, Casey busied herself with coffee, cups, and sandwiches. Dobson sat quietly at the table and waited with his hat on the floor beside him.

"I thought we might as well have lunch," Casey said.

"I'm obliged, ma'am. It's about hungry time, all right. I sent the men to eat."

What a strange man, Casey thought, and seated herself across the table from him. She waited and hoped that he would speak, but he silently and deliberately concentrated on the food before him. When he was finished, she spoke again.

"Mr. Dobson, you have taught me a great deal and I appreciate it. But like you said, it's not really your job. I have to ask, though. I mean, well you seem so knowledge-able for a freighter . . ."

When she saw the look of sadness cross his face, Casey wished she hadn't spoken. She held her breath while he looked at her, then at his plate.

"I was in business once. That was before . . . well, I was in business once."

Dobson retrieved his hat from the floor and rose.

"I'll be going now, ma'am. Thanks for the lunch and good luck to you."

Casey opened the door for the man, then followed him through it. She stared at his broad back as he walked through the wide door of the barn and stood looking up and down the street.

She turned to re-enter the barn when a movement from the group of men at the blacksmith shop caught her eye. She stopped and waited while the man who had detached himself from the group moved toward Dobson.

He walks like a gunfighter, she thought. She studied the man closely. He has an insolent slouch. His holster is worn, slung low, and tied to his leg. His clothes are dirty and his boots are worn out. He sure looks like a gunfighter down on his luck. "But what can he want with Dobson?" Casey asked herself.

She watched and waited while the man stopped in the street, set himself, spread his feet, and looked Dobson up and down.

Casey started at the sound of the voice from the backsmith shop.

"Go ahead, Willie!"

What can they want? What on earth is happening? Then Judson Wingate's words rang in her mind: "When you see a man set himself that way, something is about to happen. Get ready."

She gasped as the feeling of the imminence of sudden death paralyzed her for a moment. Then, without thinking, she carefully spread her feet, bent her knees, and let her stomach muscles sag. Casey waited.

The man called Willie stood still and looked at Dobson. Dobson did not move. Then the voice from the blacksmith shop came again.

"Go ahead, Willie!"

Casey looked toward the man. He grinned when he spoke.

"Anybody'd haul wire'd eat shit!"

Again the voice from the blacksmith shop.

"That's tellin' him, Willie!"

Casey stood with her belly slumped and watched Willie's hand spread like a claw and move slowly to a position just over his weapon.

"I'm not going to let him kill Dobson. I'm not," she muttered. Why is Dobson walking toward him? The words tumbled in her mind and she moved her hand closer to the .38.

"I think I can hit him from here. Why doesn't Dobson stop moving? He's going to get in my way!

Casey glanced quickly at Willie. He isn't looking at me, she thought. Then she looked back at Dobson as he began to speak.

"Did you speak to me, young man?"

Willie grinned.

"Yea. I said if you'd haul wire, you'd eat shit!"

Dobson was close now, almost face to face, and Casey saw Willie's grin begin to fade.

Dobson rolled his hat around in his hands for a moment before he spoke.

"Young man, I think there are a couple of things that you need to know."

"Yea. What's that?"

"Well, sir, for one thing, you may not have noticed that there is a lady present. And for another, I want you to know that I am not armed."

Suddenly the danger and the heavy feel of sudden death brought flashing images of the night William died and the only words she remembered from that time. "We let young Willie go first."

Casey screamed and clawed for the .38.

CHAPTER 15

"DAMN!"

Casey swore as the first slug slapped the dust in the middle of the street. She squeezed the trigger twice more and watched the spurts of dust move closer to Willie. "I'll get him with the next three," she told herself and tried to steady her aim.

Then she saw the gun in Willie's hand flash, heard the roar, and felt the bullet hit somewhere in the barn behind her. Dobson's broad back blocked her view and she quickly pointed her .38 at the ground and watched the freighter in amazement.

The hat in Dobson's hand was a weapon. The heavy felt was a blur as it slapped across Willie's face time after time. Casey stood stunned while the hat struck hard again and again. Willie's face was bloody as he tried to back away.

Dobson kept moving in. The hat slashed Willie's face until finally he threw up his arms. Dobson lifted a knee to Willie's groin and grabbed the .45. Willie fell to the street.

As she ran to Dobson's side, Casey thumbed back the hammer of the .38. "I'll get close enough this time. I can't miss him now," she growled. She stood beside Dobson and pointed the weapon at Willie's face. She felt sudden pain as a large hand closed over her wrist and the gun was torn from her grasp. Then a low voice sounded in her ear.

"The trouble is over there, now."

Casey turned and faced the group of men as they came

from the blacksmith shop. She felt the gun returned to her hand.

"Put it away; then step aside. It's my fight."

Casey took a step to one side and turned to look at Dobson. He slowly put on his hat and pushed it to the back of his head. Then, with the .45 in his hand, he turned and faced the approaching group. Casey stood still and watched the men approach, Anthony in the lead. She jerked at the snap in Dobson's voice.

"Move away, Mrs. Lee."

She moved a few steps, and time seemed to suspend itself while Dobson stood over Willie and waited for the other men to get within speaking distance.

When they faced him across Willie's form, Dobson deliberately flipped the catch and let the cylinder fall out the side of Willie's weapon. Then he held the gun pointed into the air while the bullets fell on Willie's chest.

I can't believe he's doing that, Casey thought. She moved her hand toward her .38. "If Anthony makes any kind of move, I'm going to kill him where he stands," she muttered.

When Anthony glared at Dobson, the others glared too. They looked at Willie on the ground, then at Dobson, and back to Anthony. Casey held her breath. They're waiting for some signal from Anthony, she thought.

Casey watched Anthony's shoulder for the slightest hint of movement. When she saw nothing, she glanced quickly back at Dobson. She gasped when the man held the .45 for a moment, steadying it, then dropped it directly into Willie's face. Then he took off his blood-smeared hat and turned it slowly in his hands as he spoke quietly to Anthony.

"You want something?" he asked.

Casey let her breath out and let her belly sag again. The handle of the .38 felt good in her hand as she waited for the cattleman to speak. She forced herself not to look at his face but to concentrate on the point of his shoulder as she waited for the slightest movement.

Relief flooded her when Anthony kept his hands high and reached into his shirt pocket for a cigar. She could feel a crowd gathering behind her now and she heard Mrs. Rogers's hoarse whisper.

"*Psst*! Casey! Get out of there! Come over here!"

Casey didn't respond but stood in the street with her feet spread and her hand on her weapon. She concentrated again on the point of Anthony's shoulder while Dobson slowly approached the man and waited for an answer to his question.

She could hear the voice of the fat sheriff as he approached from behind her.

"What's going on here?"

Casey watched Anthony while he bit the end from the cigar, fished in his pocket for a match, and struck it on his belt buckle.

Mrs. Rogers's voice came from behind Casey again.

"Casey!"

Casey didn't move. She waited to see if Dobson would need her help. She heard the sheriff's voice again.

"You freighters stay out of this! Stay where you are!"

She could barely see the fat man from the corner of her eye now as he faced Dobson's men. She brought her attention back to Dobson and Anthony. Dobson turned the blood-stained hat in his hand and spoke to Anthony again.

"I'll ask you once more. You want something with me?"

When Anthony slowly took the cigar from his mouth and blew smoke toward Dobson's face, Casey began to shake.

"He shouldn't have done that," she said aloud.

"Nope, I don't want anything. I just come over here to get young Willie before you killed him." Then, "Get up, Willie!"

Casey tried to control the shaking but she knew she

couldn't stop. Then she felt Mrs. Rogers's bulk beside her and heard her low voice growling in her ear.

"Dammit, Casey. Stop that! You made your play, now stick with it! I'm not going to let you stand in the street and spray bullets one minute, then collapse and shake like a schoolgirl the next. Come with me!"

Casey let the older woman take charge and they walked together toward Casey's barn. As they walked, Casey heard Dobson's voice behind her.

"Mrs. Lee!"

She stopped and turned toward the man. He stood with his hat in his hand again.

"Yes, Mr. Dobson?"

"I just wanted to say I'll be leaving now and . ."

Casey studied his face and the smile in his eyes.

"And thanks for the help."

Dobson put his hat on his head and climbed on the lead wagon.

Inside her living quarters, Casey threw herself on her bed and gave way to uncontrollable sobs. She knew Mrs. Rogers was still in the room but she didn't care. Suddenly Mrs. Rogers's voice cut through the fog that surrounded Casey.

"That's enough of that, now! Come get your coffee."

Casey raised her head and sniffed.

"Could I have the coffee over here please, Mrs. Rogers?"

"No. You may not. I have enough to do without serving coffee in bed to gunfighters. Come over here and get it."

Casey wiped her eyes with the heel of her hand, crossed the room, and seated herself across from the other woman. She picked up the cup of scalding coffee and sipped at it.

"Mrs. Rogers, I'm not a gunfighter," she said.

"Any fool could see that. You missed him three times at less than fifty feet. It's a wonder you didn't get somebody killed out there."

Casey stared into her cup.

"Mrs. Rogers, I don't understand any of it. I didn't even know what it was all about out there."

Casey waited while Mrs. Rogers rolled a cigarette and lit it, then pushed back her chair and crossed her legs.

"Why is she looking at me that way?" Casey asked herself. "She's angry with me and I don't even know why." She flinched at the tone in the older woman's voice.

"Casey, what in the name of God ever possessed you to bring barbed wire into open range country? Get rid of it."

Sudden anger flared in Casey at the woman's words. She's not trying to help me. She's giving me orders.

"I think you may be right, Mrs. Rogers. I think I'll do that."

"What will you do with the wire, Casey?" Mrs. Rogers voice was softer now.

Casey rose, went to the door and opened it, and looked down the long hallway of her barn at the stacks of wire.

"I'm going to sell every goddamn roll of this stuff, Mrs. Rogers. Then, I'm going to order some more!"

CHAPTER 16

CASEY sat by the forge, stared at the red-hot horseshoe, and patted Stranger's head.

"Buck, I don't understand. I said I'd be glad to pay you for the work."

"It ain't the pay, Miz Casey, you know that."

"Well, what is it then?"

She waited while the man put the glowing horseshoe on the anvil and pounded it into shape. He held it in front of his face and examined it closely, then plunged it into the tank of water.

"They's too many against it. I can't afford to be seen doing nothing like that for you. McCaslin made that clear last night."

Casey felt the sudden rush of blood to her face and tried to stop her next question.

"McCaslin's in town?"

"Yes, ma'am. There was kind of a meeting last night. Well, it wasn't a meeting really. Just a bunch in the saloon talked about it some."

"Talked about what?" Casey asked.

He was in town and he didn't come near me, she thought.

"Talked about wire mostly. McCaslin said you was to be let alone but not to be helped. He looked right at me when he said it."

The blacksmith slowly began to turn the handle of the forge blower.

"Of course I knowed he was talkin' for Anthony."

Casey let the rage boil. He mentioned my name in a saloon!

"Buck, he doesn't work for Anthony. He works for the Cattlemen's Association."

"Miz Casey, everybody knows that Anthony *is* the Cattlemen's Assocation. He'll do almost anything to get what he wants and he wants nearly everything he sees."

Casey sat and nursed her rage while Buck pounded out another horseshoe. He doesn't care anything at all about me, she thought. I'd like to kill him with my bare hands!

She waited until the shoe sizzled in the tank again; then she rose to her feet.

"You won't do it, then." Casey could hear her depression in her own words.

The huge man rested his tongs on the anvil.

"I didn't say that. I said I couldn't afford to be seen doing it. I don't care if they know it in their minds. I just don't want them to be able to say they seen me do it."

Casey sat back on her box.

"What is it you are telling me, Buck?"

"Well, I've been thinking about it. What if that thing just showed up all at once?"

Casey felt the excitement begin to fill her and she rose and paced the dirt floor.

"You could. You really could, couldn't you?"

"Yes, ma'am, if I done most of it here in the shop. Then I could haul it all over there at night and . . ."

Casey strode to the man and extended her hand.

"Buck, you may be the only real friend I have in this town," she said.

Stranger's nose nudged against her leg and Casey pushed it away. The nudge came again and Casey gave up.

"Buck, I've got to go feed this starving animal. Let me know what you need from me."

Inside her quarters Casey prepared the dog's food and

then fixed a pot of tea. Holding the cup in both hands, she sat with her elbows on the table and stared out the window. After finishing her tea, Casey took a can of paint and a brush from the shelf. "I'd better get to work," she said aloud. Casey wiped the board one more time, dipped the brush into the can of black paint, and began the work. When the paint ran in little streams from the bottom of each of the letters, she swore and wiped the board clean again.

"Damn, I can't seem to get the right amount of paint on this brush!"

She pushed Stranger away from her, worked the brush against the lip of the paint can, and started her lettering again.

"That's better," she muttered, and worked away making each letter as readable as possible. She bent closer to the work as the light faded. Holding the small of her back, she groaned, rose, and stepped back from the sign.

"Good Lord! No wonder I couldn't see. It's nearly dark."

She lit a lamp, held it high, and surveyed her work again. She nodded and, for a moment, was filled with a sense of satisfaction. Then the doubt that had been with her since the beginning returned.

"Stranger, I'd better be right about this or we are in real trouble."

Casey started at the knock, then crossed the room and swung the door open.

"Come in, Buck," she said.

"No, ma'am. I just come to tell you everything is ready. I'll be here about midnight. Better get some rest. It'll be a long, hard night."

"Thank you, Buck, I'll be ready."

Casey turned to the food safe, put a piece of ham between two halves of a biscuit, and then lay on her bed and ate. She rose once, took a long drink of water, blew out the lamp, and then lay on her bed again fully clothed.

She closed her eyes and tried to doze. she shifted and turned and tried to make her mind a blank.

"For God's sake, Stranger, stop pacing! Your toenails are driving me crazy."

She listened to the silence for a moment; then she felt the animal place her chin on the side of the bed. Casey patted Stranger's head.

"It's not you, Stranger. It's me. I'll be glad when this night is over."

She stroked the dog's head and tried to relax. As she stared into the darkness, the question she wanted to evade formed in her mind again. First it was a hazy word that seemed to hover in the distance and then it moved closer and closer until it overwhelmed her with its persistence. When she could resist no longer, Casey moaned into the night.

"Why?" she asked the darkness. "Why hasn't he been here? He's been in town three days now! I want him back . . . so I can send him away!"

"Ho, boy, ho."

The sound of a quiet voice and the tinkle of chain outside her window cleared the rage from Casey's mind and brought her back to the moment.

Casey struck a match and looked at the clock. It's not twelve yet. I wonder who that is? She rose and peered out the window at the dark form of a man quietly working a draft horse. She opened her door and stepped into the darkness.

"Buck! Is that you?" she whispered.

"Yes, ma'am. I started a little early. I wanted to get the stuff over here as soon as possible."

"What can I do to help?"

"Nothing yet, but you'd better get some gloves. I'll need all the help I can get before the night is over."

Casey sat on the bench with the heavy gloves in her lap, straining to see while Buck moved everything into place. When she heard his whisper, she rose and went to him.

"Did you mark the corners?" he asked.

She took his arm and led him to the place she had put the first marker stone.

"Here's the first one," she whispered.

Casey stepped back and listened to the "thug" of the posthole digger as Buck's powerful arms slammed the device into the ground.

Casey moved around the man and wished he would give her more to do. She brought the water bucket and gave him a drink from time to time; then she sat on the bench waiting for him to ask for help.

He seems slow but he's getting it done, she thought. I suppose it's because he stays so steadily at the work. When Buck paused to rest, she tried to help with the tamping but found she could hardly lift the heavy iron bar.

When the posts were set and braced, Casey spoke again, in a whisper.

"Can I get you something to eat, Buck?"

"There's no time for that. Let's get the wire."

Casey struggled to help with the rolls of wire and the other equipment. They worked with their faces close to the wire now. He seems so sure of himself, Casey thought. Why am I so confused? I don't think I understand how that stretcher works at all.

She waited while Buck aligned the ropes of the stretcher and pulled the wire tight. When she heard his muffled "Now," she put a heavy staple in place and pounded it with the hammer.

"It takes forever to pound in these things," she muttered. "We'll never get it done by daylight."

She glanced over her shoulder at the tiny crescent of pink that showed in the east and pounded harder with the hammer. Hammer in hand, she waited again for Buck's "Now," put another staple in place, and brought the hammer crashing down on her fingers.

"Damn! Damn!"

Casey jammed the fingers in her mouth and stood sucking on them while Buck held the tension on the wire and waited for her. She smelled the familiar male odor of Red McCaslin as he took the hammer from her hand.

Casey didn't speak. She simply moved to the bench and sat and waited to see what would happen. She watched and waited as the two men worked silently and efficiently, as a team. They were dark shadows against the light of early day.

Casey rose, went inside, and began to prepare breakfast. When it was ready, she opened the door and spoke one word.

"Breakfast."

Buck came to her.

"It's all done, Miz Casey. I have to go now."

"Mr. McCaslin, will you have breakfast? It seems the least I could do for a man who stays up all night and is reckless with his money."

Casey walked to the stove as McCaslin came through the door. She spoke over her shoulder.

"Have a seat, Mr. McCaslin. I'll serve you shortly."

She slammed the plate onto the table before him and tried to feel nothing as the man looked at her.

"What do you mean, reckless with my money?"

"Well, you paid that boy a whole ten cents to come tell me you'd be here three days ago and I haven't seen you till you came sneaking up behind me in the dark. Seems to me you wasted your dime."

When McCaslin frowned, pushed away the plate of food, and rose, Casey caught her breath.

McCaslin's voice was low and the words came slowly: "Casey, there is more going on and more trouble than you have any idea of. I'll explain it all when I can..." McCaslin's arms closed around her and then her feet were floating above the floor.

CHAPTER 17

CASEY lay close to Red McCaslin with her head on his shoulder. She slowly moved her hand through the short curly hair on his chest.

"I'll see the preacher today," he said.

"Preacher? What for?"

"To get us married. What else?"

Casey sucked in her breath and held it as long as possible. When she could hold it no longer, she exhaled slowly.

"I can't do that, Red."

"What do you mean, you can't do it? Why not?"

"I'm not ready."

"I don't understand. You were ready enough a little while ago."

Casey moved away from him a little.

"That has nothing to do with anything. I have very important things to do."

"Such as . . ."

"For one thing, I have a barn full of wire to sell."

She felt his body stiffen.

"Wire? Wire? For God's sake, can't you think of anything but wire? It's the worse thing you could have done, bringing that wire in here. We'll have to get rid of that right away."

Casey sat up abruptly. She felt herself flush as Red looked at her and she carefully covered one of her breasts before she spoke.

"Red McCaslin, it's time somebody told me why there is so much excitement about my wire. It's good, it's cheap, and nearly everybody in this country could use some of it."

"I'll show you what all the fuss is about!"

Casey gasped as McCaslin threw back the cover and rolled from the bed. He stood before her for a moment. Then he began to turn in a circle before her.

"See that? See those scars? That's what wire is good for."

Casey groaned. "Oh Red! When did you get those?"

"About a year ago. Rode into it at a full lope on a dark night. Some fool homesteader . . . The wire broke and we went down. That bloody tangle of horse, wire, and me taught me all I need to know."

She felt his anger fill the room as he spoke again.

"Have you ever heard a horse scream, Casey?"

Casey lay back and pulled the light cover up to her chin. He's so angry, she thought. Everybody gets so angry when they talk about wire. He has really been hurt, though; that's plain to see.

She said nothing while the man dressed. When he was fully clothed, she rose from the bed, wrapped the coverlet around her, and crossed the room to where McCaslin stood with his hand on the doorknob.

"You don't want me to see the preacher, then?" he asked.

Casey shook her head slowly.

"I'm not going to be your wife, Red." She paused. ". . . and I'm not going to be your whore, either. Don't get any ideas from what happened here this morning."

Casey stood with the cover draped around her and studied the puzzled look on McCaslin's face. When he turned and opened the door, Casey spoke again.

"Red?"

He turned to face her and Stranger squeezed past him into the room through the open crack of the door.

"Yes, Casey?"

"Red, do you think the wire hurts an animal any more

than men do when they rope him, brand him, and cut his balls out?"

She smiled at the slammed door and the sound of Red's voice growling on the other side.

"Son of a bitch!"

Casey hummed as she dressed, then moved about her quarters straightening things. She made the bed, smoothed it carefully, and then patted it gently. She felt the smile spread across her face as the memory of the early morning hours went through her mind. The sound of voices outside broke her reverie and she snapped herself out of the mood and spoke aloud.

"Casey Lee, you are the biggest fool in Texas."

Then she moved the curtain aside and peeked out the window at the group of men gathered around the structure she and Buck had labored through the night to build.

She turned to the table, picked up a biscuit, and tossed it to Stranger.

"We'll let them wait and wonder for a while, Stranger; then we'll put up the sign."

Casey lay on the bed for a long time and listened to the murmur of voices outside.

"They're curious, all right," she told herself. "Maybe it's time to put up the sign."

She rose and crossed the room to where the sign sat on edge on a straight chair. She touched the tip of a finger to one of the letters and then looked at the finger. When she saw no paint on herself, she took a hammer and a handful of nails from the shelf.

She opened the door, picked up the heavy sign, and walked outside. She stopped short when she saw the size of the crowd of men and a few women.

"Every one of them is really looking my pen over, especially that one little old man," she told herself. "This thing may work out for me."

She nodded and smiled at the people as she carried her sign to the wire enclosure. She put the hammer on the ground and held the wooden sign against one of the corner posts, setting the sign quickly on the ground when its weight became too much for her. Casey raised the sign again and looked over her shoulder in a silent plea for help. When no one moved toward her, she started to put the sign down again. Then she heard Mrs. Rogers's voice on her left.

"Let me hold that for you, Casey."

Casey surrendered the load to Mrs. Rogers. Mrs. Rogers jammed the sign against the corner post and Casey stepped back to survey its position.

"A little lower, Mrs. Rogers. There, that's it."

Casey returned and drove a nail through the boards and into the post. Then she stepped back again and made arm-waving motions to Mrs. Rogers until the sign was straight. When she was satisfied, she drove in the other nails. Then she and Mrs. Rogers stood with arms folded and examined what they'd done.

"Casey, you are the craziest white woman I have ever met. One or two Indians, maybe, were crazier but you are definitely the craziest white woman."

Casey laughed.

"I believe you," she said.

The voice behind her startled Casey and she spun on her heel to face the little man.

"Young lady, does that sign say what they say it says?"

"Yes, sir, it means exactly what it says."

"Read it to me."

Puzzled, Casey stared at the work-worn face for a moment.

"I ain't the only one around here that can't read," he said. "Read the sign to me."

Casey felt a surge of embarrassment as Mrs. Rogers's stage whisper struck her ears.

"Read the sign, Casey. That's Harold Grimley. He can't read!"

I wish she'd shut up. I know he must have heard that, Casey thought. She turned and faced the sign, then looked at the man beside her.

"Sir, the sign reads, One Hundred Dollars Free to the Owner of Any Bull That Can Get Out of This Pen. Then, at the bottom, I have signed my name. The sign means exactly what it says."

Casey paused and studied the man again.

"Do you have a mean bull, sir?"

"I think I have."

"Would you like to bring him in and try him in the pen? If he can get out, I'll definitely pay the hundred dollars."

"I can feel something here," Casey told herself. "I'm not sure what. The way Mrs. Rogers said his name . . ."

"No, miss, I don't think I'll bring my bull in. I'll be in town a couple of days. I'll wait."

Casey felt disappointment as the man turned to leave. Somehow, what had seemed to be an important conversation had trailed off into nothing. She wanted to keep the discussion going but she could think of nothing further to say. As the man turned away, the words seemed to come to her without thought.

"Wait for what?"

The man turned back and smiled at her.

"Lady, there are men around here that would choke a baby for a dime. I'll be around town for awhile. It won't be long till you'll see some young bucks come riding in. They will have four or five ropes on some mean bull. They will try for your hundred dollars."

The little man looked down at his boots.

"I'll learn all I need to know about your wire then."

Casey stood blinking in the sunlight as the little man touched his hat, turned on his heel, and walked away. She turned to ask Mrs. Rogers more about the man. All she could see was the woman's broad back as she hurried toward her store.

CHAPTER 18

CASEY walked around her special pen and looked it over.

"It seems good and strong," she told herself. "But if one bull ever gets out of there, I'm done for."

She opened the gate and looked at the heavy handmade hinges. She closed the gate and dropped the strong latch in place, then turned and walked toward Rogers's store. Most of the men lounging on the benches in front of the store touched their hats when she mounted the boardwalk.

Mr. Grimley didn't even see me, Casey thought. He's just staring at my pen. She went inside and moved idly about the store while Mrs. Rogers waited on other customers. When the woman noticed her, Casey shook her head.

"I'm in no hurry, Mrs. Rogers. Take your time."

Casey wandered to the door and stood looking through the screen into the street. A movement caught her eye and she glanced toward her barn and at the lone man circling her test pen.

"Why, that's Anthony," she murmured. "I wonder what he's up to? Good Lord! Stranger's trying to drive him away!"

She watched Stranger follow Anthony as he slowly circled the pen. She could see Stranger's teeth and she knew that she must be growling too.

Casey gasped as Anthony whirled and landed a hard kick in Stranger's side.

"Damn! He's kicked my dog!" she said aloud.

She slammed herself out the door and into the dirt street and ran toward her barn. I hope she's not hurt bad, she thought.

Casey stopped a few feet from Anthony.

"That was my dog you kicked, mister."

Anthony glanced toward the entrance of the barn.

"She ran in there," he said.

"I know that. Why did you kick her?"

"She acted like she wanted to bite me."

Casey tried to calm herself but her fury grew. She felt her hand inch toward the weapon on her hip. Suddenly all the fear and rage left her. There was nothing now but an icy calm as she listened to her own words.

"I see you're armed, Anthony."

Casey felt the man's surprise as he snapped himself erect.

"You want to fight me?"

"You're armed, aren't you?"

Casey waited as Anthony glanced toward the loungers in front of Rogers's store and then back to her.

"I'm not going to fight a woman. I'd never live it down."

"Mister, you're not even going to live through it. You don't have any choice. You are either going to have to fight me, or every one of those gawkers in front of that store is going to see you faced down by a woman."

Casey watched the man closely as he took a cigar from his shirt pocket and then spoke again: "Young woman, do you know who I am?"

"I know exactly who you are. I know that you are doing everything you can to cause me trouble and I may as well kill you now as later."

She was breathing hard now and she wished her icy calm would return and that Anthony were not so calm.

"Young woman, if you're going to shoot me, you are going to have to stand out here in front of all those people and shoot me in the back."

Anthony lit the cigar.

"I'm not going to draw on you. In fact, I am going to turn my back and walk away," he said.

My God! What do I do now? Casey thought. I can't just stand here and shoot him in the back. She drew herself up as tall as possible and spoke as Anthony turned his back.

"Mr. Anthony! I give you fair warning. If you ever touch that dog, or anything else of mine, again . . ." She tried to keep the force in her voice but she could hear it trailing off miserably, ". . . you'll answer to me."

The voice behind her came as a shock and Casey whirled to face it.

"If you're not going to shoot the man, maybe we could talk some."

Casey looked into the face of Harold Grimley. She stood speechless for a moment and then stammered.

"What is it you want to talk about, Mr. Grimley?"

When Grimley raised his arm and pointed down the street, Casey shaded her eyes with her hand. "What's he pointing at?" she asked herself. Then she saw the cloud of dust approaching town and Grimley's voice sounded behind her: "There ain't no doubt in my mind what's causing that cloud of dust."

"What is it, Mr. Grimley?"

Casey felt Anthony's presence as the man moved to stand beside them; then she heard his low laugh as he spoke.

"Well, we'll learn something now."

Casey ignored Anthony's remark and waited for Grimley to speak again.

"That there has got to be some fellers coming to collect your hundred dollars, missy."

Casey felt the fear as it shot through her body and she had to force a calmness into her voice.

"Well, I certainly hope so, Mr. Grimley." Then to herself, "He acted like he didn't even hear me."

"If that pen holds that bull till tomorrow morning, I will want five hundred rolls of your wire."

"Five hundred!" Casey gasped. Lord! If I can start off that big, she thought.

Then Anthony's voice boomed in her ear.

"Grimley, you're not going to do that!"

"I'm going to do it if this pen holds the Stanton bull."

Casey looked as Grimley nodded toward the two riders who had reached the end of the street. Their horses strained as the large bull pulled backward against the ropes around his horns. Then the riders spurred their mounts forward to take up the slack as the bull ran a few steps and then stopped to fight the ropes again.

When the riders reached the pen, Casey moved out of the way while they shortened their ropes, then moved in opposite directions until the ropes were tight, holding the animal helpless.

Casey nodded when one of the riders took off his hat and spoke to her.

"We're the Stanton brothers, ma'am. We come to get your hundred dollars."

The rider put his hat back on his head and lounged in his saddle grinning.

Casey looked at the bull as he stood pawing the ground. She took a deep breath and cursed the weakness in her knees.

"Put him in the pen," she said. "If he gets out by tomorrow morning with no help, I'll pay the hundred. Fair?"

The man grinned and nodded. Casey walked away from the pen and sat on the bench. She made room when Grimley joined her and neither spoke until the bull had been dragged into the pen. Casey wished Anthony would leave but he stood to one side and waited until the Stantons had closed the heavy gate.

Casey watched the bull carefully. When the ropes were off, he stood seemingly stunned at the sudden freedom. He looked to the right. He's looking right at me, Casey thought. I wonder if he is blaming me for his trouble. The bull swung his head to the left and pawed the ground.

"What's the matter with him, Bill? I ain't never seen him act like that."

The other Stanton laughed.

"Don't you worry about him. You just get ready to spend that hundred."

Casey kept her eyes on the bull. She could feel a crowd

gathering, but beyond that she hardly knew the people were there. She concentrated on the bull as he pawed the ground and sent spurts of dust as his hoofs dug at the loose dirt.

Without warning, the animal stopped his pawing and walked directly into the wire between the heavy posts. Casey held her breath while the wire squeaked as it strained against the posts. The posts creaked and Casey trembled inside and waited for the bull's next move.

He backed away from the fence and stood pawing again. Casey could see drops of blood forming on the animal's nose and face. She glanced sideways at Grimley and she could tell he was intently studying the entire scene.

I wonder if he is concerned about the bull or the fence? she thought. Then, without warning, the bull charged the corner post.

"My God, he's cracked the post!" Casey groaned as she heard the sharp sound. The bull stood still for a moment, front legs spread and head lowered. He raised his head, swung it from right to left, and began to back away from the post. Casey held her breath and waited. The bull backed the length of the pen until his buttocks pushed hard against the barbs behind him. Casey clenched her fists as the animal bellowed and charged the post again. She closed her eyes and listened to the sound of the animal's head crashing again and again against the heavy post.

"There goes my last hundred dollars," she told herself and waited for the sound of laughter from the crowd.

Suddenly the sounds stopped. Casey squeezed her eyes tighter and waited and listened. The only sound she could hear now over the murmur of the crowd was the sound of the bull's heavy breathing.

"Young lady, could you wake up long enough to talk business?"

Casey opened her eyes and turned to Harold Grimley.

"I want five hundred rolls of your wire, miss. I'll pay now. I'll send for it in a few days."

"Well, ah, yes, of course, but . . ."

"But what, ma'am?"

Casey looked at the Stanton bull, standing, and dripping blood.

"Didn't you want to wait till you see if the Stanton bull . . ."

Casey followed Grimley's gaze back to the bull.

"I've seen enough. I want the wire."

"Well, come inside and . . ."

Casey jerked as Anthony's voice cut in.

"No you don't, Grimley. You know the association's position on wire. You're not buying that wire."

Casey stepped aside as Anthony's hand fell on Grimley's shoulder and spun him around. She waited to see what would happen.

"Take your hand off me, Anthony." Grimley's voice was low and slow as he spoke. "The association is wrong."

Casey covered her mouth with her hand and watched the two men as Anthony removed his hand and stepped back.

"You're not going to fence that boundary. I'll see to that."

Casey could feel the force in Grimley's voice as he answered. He's so small for that, she thought.

"I'm not saying what I'm going to fence. It's my business."

Casey let her breath out slowly.

"I hope he doesn't change his mind. Oh I hope . . ." she murmured.

She let the feeling of relief begin to flow through her when Anthony turned to walk away; then she gasped at the shock of his words as the man turned back to Grimley and shook his fist.

"McCaslin will be around to see you!"

CHAPTER 19

GRIMLEY took a bandanna from his pocket, took off his hat, and wiped his forehead. Then he put the hat back on.

"Anthony, I'll talk to anybody, but I'm here to tell you there ain't a man in Texas that is going to tell me what to do."

Grimley looked at Casey, then walked to her front door and waited for her to follow. She felt her heart pound as she joined the man at the door.

"This your office, ma'am?"

Casey nodded, opened the door, went inside, held the door open, and waited for Grimley to follow. She motioned Grimley to a chair at her table and then rummaged for a pen and a sheet of paper.

"I suppose I should list what you want," she said.

"Yes, ma'am, that's the thing to do. I'll need the wire and enough staples to put it up." He hesitated a moment.

"And if it's all right, I'd like to borrow a stretcher, and somebody will have to show me how to work that."

Casey tried to stop the panic she felt at Grimley's remark.

"I wonder if I remember anything at all about that stretcher?" she asked herself.

She smiled and began to write.

"I'm not sure I remember all about that, but I'm sure you can figure it out . . . or Buck can tell you."

Casey hesitated a moment, then spoke quietly.

"If he'll tell you," she said.

She looked across the table at Grimley and felt relieved when she saw he was smiling.

"He'll tell me," the man said.

Casey listed the wire and then wrote down, "Two kegs of staples."

"I'm listing two kegs of staples, Mr. Grimley. If that's too many, you can return what you don't need."

She glanced at the man. When he nodded, she totaled the bill.

"That comes to one thousand and ten dollars," she said.

Casey mentally counted with him as Grimley counted out the money. She stuffed the money into her pocket. When Mr. Grimley rose to leave, Casey waited for a moment and then spoke, "Mr. Grimley, would you tell me why Mr. Anthony was so dead set to stop you from buying this wire?"

"Oh, Anthony's all right, I guess. He just wants to run everything around here, is all."

"But he seemed so outraged that it was you buying the wire. It seemed to mean a great deal to him."

"Well, yes, I guess it does. You see, his place joins mine. We've argued some for years. Now it's about the water. Most of the water is on my place. He's afraid I'll fence him out of it."

Casey nodded and followed Grimley to the door. As he went out, she spoke again.

"Mr. Grimley, will you? I mean, will you fence him away from the water?"

Casey waited while the man seemed to consider her question for a long time before he spoke.

"Has Anthony ever offered to buy your place?"

Casey shook her head.

"Strange. I would if I was him."

Casey felt a little stunned by the question, and while she tried to think what to say next, Grimley touched his hat and walked away.

"I wonder what that was all about," she murmured, as she leaned out the door to look for Stranger. She looked to the right and to the left. I wonder where she could be? Casey walked the length of the barn looking in each stall and calling, "Stranger! Come!"

"I hope she's not really hurt," she told herself. As she passed the stacks of wire, she let a happy feeling flow through her as she enjoyed the thought of the nice sale to Grimley.

I wonder how I can get the money to the Glidden Company to pay for the wire? There's no bank here. Leedy's just too small. I'd be afraid to ride all the way to Abilene with this much money. Casey pondered the question as she went inside. She paced the length of the room several times, then seated herself at the table, picked up the pen and paper, and began to write.

Dear Mr. Glidden:

I have sold five hundred rolls of your wire. Here is the money to pay for it. I hope to be able to sell some more soon.

If I am fortunate enough to do that, I will be in short supply. Please send me five hundred more rolls of the wire and some more staples.

Sincerely,
C. Lee

Casey read and reread the letter and listened to her mother's words from the past: "Casey, a letter is important. It is a projection of yourself. You must always make sure that each letter you write is correct in every way."

Sadness filled her as she thought of her mother. It's been so long since I heard from her, she thought. I wish she would write more often.

She scanned the letter again.

"It's not fancy," she said under her breath. "But it says what I wanted to say." She went to the kitchen cabinet, opened the doors, and stared at the contents. She took down a can labeled "Royal Baking Powder" and studied it. Then she nodded and dumped the contents into a small bowl. She wiped the inside with a dry cloth and put the can on the table beside her letter. She counted out $505 and stuffed the money into the can. Then she worked the letter in beside the money. Casey looked at the arrangement and frowned. "It worries me," she told herself. She took a sheet of writing paper, crumpled it, and forced it into the can on top of the letter and money. Then she carried the can to the cabinet and carefully ladled baking powder back into the can until it was full. She put the lid on the can and then found a candle and dripped wax around the top to seal the can.

'Well, it's sealed in there pretty good," she told herself. "Now if I can get it sent off."

She wrapped the can in heavy brown paper and tied it with strong string. Then she wrote the address on the paper wrapping.

Casey took the small package and started out the door. Gusts of wind swirled dust around her and into her eyes and she hurried to reach Rogers's store.

Mrs. Rogers looked up from behind the counter and nodded as the wind slammed the door behind Casey.

"What brings you out in the wind, Casey?"

"I've got a little package here. Will you get it on the first mail that runs?"

The older woman took the round package, collected the postage from Casey, and tossed the package into the outgoing mail sack.

Casey heard the door slam in the wind behind her and turned to see who the customer might be.

"Grimley buy the wire?" the man asked.

When Casey didn't answer, the man took off his hat and stood before her, embarrassed.

"I didn't mean to pry none. It's, well, my name is Jones, ma'am. I think you know my boy. I work for Mr. Grimley some and I was hopin' he done it. He likely would need me to help him with it and I could use the work."

Casey nodded.

"He bought the wire and I hope you get the work."

"Thank you, ma'am."

As the man turned to leave, Casey called after him.

"You have a nice boy, Mr. Jones."

She turned back to Mrs. Rogers.

"Will you let me know when the mail has gone out?"

"Yes, Casey, it should go out in a day or two."

The woman turned away and then, her mouth set in a grim line, suddenly turned back to Casey.

"Casey, you really don't know what you've done, do you?"

Casey raised her eyebrows and waited for Mrs. Rogers to say more.

"You surely know that that wire sale to Grimley will start all kinds of trouble around here. I had hoped . . ."

Casey felt the anger flash and she made no effort to control it. She slapped the countertop as hard as she could with her open hand.

"Trouble! Trouble? Am I the only person in the state of Texas that's supposed to have trouble? I've done nothing but struggle with my troubles since I got here. Yet every time I turn around, somebody is saying something like that to me."

Casey paused for breath and then went on: "Will you kindly tell me what is so terrible about me selling wire? Why is that so different than for you to sell hammers, or yard goods?" The look on Mrs. Rogers's face softened as she saw Casey struggling to control her anger.

Casey clung to the counter until she was calm.

"You're a good friend, Mrs. Rogers. I don't know what I would do without you."

Casey let herself out the door into the windswept twilight and hurried back to her barn. "She worries me with her prying and bossiness but I like her," she told herself.

Casey laid out a cold supper, and as she put the biscuits on the table, she reached for one to toss to Stranger. I sure enjoy those nudges against my leg, she thought. She put the biscuit back on the plate, then opened the door and shouted into the rising wind, "Stranger! Come! Come on girl!"

When the dog didn't appear, Casey whistled several times, then listened to see if she could hear an answering bark. When she heard nothing but the wind and the sound of Maude, restless in her stall, she went out and closed the big barn doors and went back into her quarters.

She ate her cold supper, undressed, and went to bed. She lay and listened to the sound of the wind and of Maude in her stall, and hoped that Stranger would scratch at the door soon.

In the night when she felt the change, she waited a long time and listened to the night sounds. What's different? she thought. Slowly the different sound invaded her mind. The irregular thudding began to separate itself from the usual sounds of the barn in the wind.

Casey rose, struck a match, and found a lantern. She lit the lantern and went out the door into the hallway of the barn. "It's coming from out front," she told herself and moved closer to the big doors.

She put her palm against the door. She could feel a movement shake the door at each thudding sound.

Casey put the lantern on the floor, removed the heavy bar, and pushed against the door. When the door resisted, she picked up the lantern and put her back against the door and pushed hard with both feet against the wind pressure. The door moved a little; then as the wind slackened, it slowly opened.

Casey went through the door, turned, and held the lantern high. She gasped as the pale light shone on the red dog, hung from a nail in the door by a length of barbed wire around her neck. Casey retched when she saw the slit belly and the entrails hanging between the dog's hind legs as the wind beat the animal's body against the door.

"Stranger! Stranger!"

Casey crouched on the ground under her dead dog, beat the hard ground again and again with her fists, and let her screams fill the night.

CHAPTER 20

CASEY rested her bandaged hands on the counter.

"Do you have a shotgun, Mr. Smalley?"

"Yes, I have several. What on earth happened to . . ."

Casey cut the question short.

"Is it true that a shotgun scatters the shot?"

"Yes, ma'am. Sometimes they call them scatterguns."

"Is it also true that if the barrel of a shotgun is shortened that the shot covers such a wide area that it is almost impossible to miss with it?"

"I'd say so, yes."

Casey cupped her aching left hand in her right.

"That's what I want."

She watched the furrow between the gunsmith's eyes.

"Mrs. Lee, I'm not sure I understand exactly what it is you're asking for."

He's stalling, she thought. He doesn't want to sell me the gun.

Casey sighed.

"Mr. Smalley, what I am asking for is a sawed-off shotgun."

Casey tried to ignore the man's stare at her hands.

"Well, I need to know more than that. I need to know what gauge, how short you want it, how much you are willing to pay . . ."

Casey held up a hand to stop the man's flow of words.

"Let me put it this way, Mr. Smalley. If you wanted to kill

a man at short range . . . ," Casey glanced at the rack of guns, "which one of those would you saw off to use?"

Casey waited while the man stared at her for a moment. Then he turned to the gun rack and took a double-barreled shotgun from it. He put it on the counter before him.

"Mrs. Lee, if I sawed off the barrel of this weapon as short as possible, and if you were as close as you are talking about, it would probably kill whoever you pointed it at and injure anyone else who wasn't standing behind the gun."

Casey could see the worry in the man's eyes as he leaned on the counter and stared at her over the top of his glasses.

"That is exactly what I had in mind. Get it ready. I'll be back in two hours."

The man picked up the weapon and Casey turned to leave. As she reached the door, he called after her.

"It will be kind of expensive."

Casey answered the question she could hear in the man's voice.

"Just get it ready," she said.

Casey trudged down the empty street to her barn. Inside she took the teakettle from the stove and poured hot water into a wash pan. She carefully unwrapped her hands and eased them into the hot water.

She winced at the pain and spoke aloud.

"God damn 'em, Stranger! Somebody is going to pay for all they have done to us!"

When the water began to cool, she carefully dried her bruised hands and tried to flex her fingers.

"I've really done it this time," she told herself. "But I've got to make them work. I'm completely helpless this way."

She carefully took the .38 from its holster and unloaded it. Then she put the weapon back in the holster and forced herself to draw.

"Too slow and clumsy," she told herself and tried again.

Casey swore as the weapon fell to the floor on the second try.

"Damn! I was right. I've got to have that shotgun."

She reloaded the .38 and put it back in its holster. She adjusted the gun belt to its most comfortable position and retied the bottom of the holster to her leg. Then she glanced at the clock on the wall.

"Smalley won't have that thing ready for another hour," she muttered.

She paced the floor and flexed her fingers as she paced.

"The pain is a little better now," she told herself.

She went out the door and sauntered over to the blacksmith shop. Buck nodded and spat a stream of tobacco juice into the forge. Casey seated herself on the wooden box near the anvil and waited for Buck to plunge the glowing iron into the water tank before she spoke.

"Buck?"

"Yes, Miz Casey."

"If you wanted to shoot somebody with a shotgun, what size shot would you use?"

The blacksmith withdrew the iron from the water tank, held the iron up and examined it closely, then carefully put it into the fire again. Casey waited for him to speak. He's not going to answer me, she thought. Buck spat into the forge again and then spoke, "Cripple or kill?"

Casey snapped her answer and was a little surprised at the harshness of her tone.

"Kill," she said.

Casey waited while Buck shifted the piece of iron in the coals and seemed to consider his answer.

"You find out who done that to Stranger?"

"I think I know."

"You think?"

"I know," Casey grated.

"You killin' sure?"

"I'm sure enough."

Casey rose to her feet as Buck began to turn the blower handle. "I may as well leave," she told herself. She hesitated when Buck stopped turning the handle and poked at the iron in the fire.

"If I was killin' sure, I'd use double-aught buckshot," he said.

Casey nodded and walked out of the shop and down the street. Without thinking she crossed the street as she approached the saloon and walked along the other side toward the gun shop. At the gunsmith's door, she turned and looked toward the saloon. She silently cursed herself as her heart jumped at the sight of McCaslin's horse tied at the rail.

"The very idea! Just because his horse is there. I think I hate that man!"

Still looking at the horse, she pushed open the door of the gun shop and stepped directly into the arms of Red McCaslin.

"It's him. Damn, damn, damn, it's him!" she said to herself.

Casey pushed herself away.

"How do you do, Mr. McCaslin?"

"Hello, Casey, I just got into town."

Casey glanced over her shoulder through the open door at the stallion across the street and said nothing.

". . . a couple of hours ago," he said.

Casey moved to step around McCaslin.

"That's nice," she said.

She walked to the counter and spoke to the gunsmith. "Is it ready?"

She followed Smalley's quick glance toward McCaslin before he spoke.

"Well no, not exactly, you see . . . well, Red, he seems to think that . . ."

McCaslin was beside her now with his hand on her shoulder.

"I told him not to fix the shotgun for you."

Casey tried to fight back the rage and to find the words

she wanted. McCaslin's voice was soft when he began again.

"I heard about Stranger," he said.

My God! My knees are going to buckle, she thought.

"Take your hand off me, Red McCaslin!"

Casey dropped her shoulder and stepped back as his hand fell away. She turned back to the gunsmith.

"Mr. Smalley, you agreed to sell me that weapon and to modify it to my specifications."

She could hardly breathe now and she was afraid she couldn't finish what she had to say.

"I am sure you are a man of your word, so I am going to wait right here till the gun is finished. I expect to see that weapon on that counter along with two boxes of double-aught buckshot in the next twenty minutes."

With the delivery of the speech, she began to breathe better and her anger began to subside, only to return when Smalley glanced at McCaslin, obviously seeking his permission.

When McCaslin nodded to the gunsmith, her rage increased.

"Goddammit, Smalley! This man doesn't have anything to do with my affairs. Don't look to him for permission when I make a request!"

Casey tapped her foot and waited until the gunsmith took the shotgun from the rack, clamped it in a vise, and reached for a hacksaw.

Then she took a deep breath and turned to McCaslin, all the while hating the feeling she got in her body when she looked at the man.

"Mr. McCaslin, I want to make myself perfectly clear. It is going to be absolutely necessary that you never meddle in my affairs again. If you do . . ."

Casey paused, drew another deep breath, and tried to decide how to finish her speech.

"A dog isn't a killing matter," he said.

Casey stamped her foot.

"That depends entirely on whose dog it was! I can't see *you* standing still for a thing like that! They tell around here that you shot a man for whipping his own horse."

Casey heard the low chuckle behind her and she whirled to face the gunsmith.

"Mr. Smalley, this is not a laughing matter and I'll thank you to stay out of it."

That's better, she thought as the gunsmith assumed a serious expression. She turned back to McCaslin.

"That dog was the only thing in this world that I had that I could feel sure of and I'm not going to let the matter drop."

His soft voice seemed to fill the room.

"Casey, you don't even know who did it."

"I know all right. He warned Grimley yesterday that he was going to order you to call on him about the wire he bought."

Casey gasped at the look that came onto McCaslin's face and she watched him struggle to control himself.

"That horrible look. It's the last thing some men have ever seen on this earth," she told herself.

Casey heard the soft sound as Smalley put the weapon on the counter behind her and then the plop, plop as he put the two boxes of shells beside it. She turned away from McCaslin.

"Show me how to load it," she said to Smalley.

She watched carefully while the man flipped the lever and broke open the shotgun, took two shells from the box, and inserted them in the chambers.

Casey could feel McCaslin moving behind her and she could hear him breathing hard. She reached for the weapon where Smalley held it still open in his hand. She took the weapon and hefted it in her hand as the voice came from behind her.

"Casey! Nobody, not even *you*, talks to me like . . ."

Casey snapped the barrels shut and cocked both hammers as she whirled and pointed the weapon at McCaslin's middle.

"Understand this, McCaslin! I have a business to run and a living to make. None of this has anything to do with you. Don't come around me and don't try to intimidate my customers."

Casey tightened her grip on the short shotgun and pain shot through her hand as her fingers took up the slack in the triggers.

"Now get out of my way before I blow you in two with this thing!"

CHAPTER 21

CASEY sat at the table with her head on her arms and pushed the shotgun away from her.

My God, I was close to killing him, she thought. These fools around here don't seem to understand anything else, though. Why do I stay here?

She buried her head deeper in her arms and let the tears begin. I won't. I won't be put through this, day after day. I'll go home. I'll go home to Mother. I'll write her tonight. I know she'll let me come. I know she will!

Casey sat for a long time and thought of her mother and of the older woman's comforting arms.

Casey tried to ignore the sound of a team outside. Pounding on the door forced her to return to the present and she rose and opened the door to Harold Grimley.

"Me and Jones have come for the wire."

"Just pull your wagon inside the barn and go ahead and start loading," she said. "We can count together as you load."

Grimley motioned to the man on the wagon. Casey went inside and found a pencil and joined the men at the stacks of wire.

"Any particular stack?" Grimley asked.

"No. Just start anyplace."

Casey walked to one of the stall partitions.

"I'll make a mark on this board for each roll you load. When you have five hundred, I'll let you know."

When the men nodded and started to work, Casey watched carefully, making sure she made an accurate count.

I'm glad Mr. Dobson took the time to teach me a little about this, she thought.

When the wagon was loaded, Grimley approached her.

"I count two fifty," he said. "Looks like that's all the wagon will hold. This will get us started. I'll come for the rest later."

Casey counted her marks and nodded.

"That's what I count too, Mr. Grimley. I'm never very far away from here. You can come for the rest of it any time."

Casey stood aside while Grimley mounted the wagon and Jones backed the team out of the barn.

"Heard you had a set-to with McCaslin."

Casey turned to face Mrs. Rogers.

"Oh, I didn't hear you come in," Casey said. "Do you know everything that happens in this town?"

"I try. Are you going to offer me tea and tell me about it or are you just going to stand out here and gloat over all that money you made selling wire?"

Casey smiled.

"Serve tea, of course, Mrs. Rogers. Come on inside."

Inside Casey moved the shotgun from the table, prepared the tea, served Mrs. Rogers, and then seated herself.

"What happened with you and McCaslin? It's all over town you threatened to kill him."

Casey hesitated.

"Well, I guess I did. I didn't intend to really do it, though. Did he tell you about it?"

Mrs. Rogers laughed.

"No, not that one. He doesn't tell much of anything to anybody. Mrs. Smalley told me right after noon. Smalley told her when he came home to lunch. Like I said, it's all over town."

Casey sipped her tea and then sighed.

"Mrs. Rogers, that man drives me crazy butting in the way he does. I can't stand him. I've got to get rid of him some way."

"I don't believe I'd kill him, Casey."

"Oh, for heaven's sake, I'm not going to kill him."

Casey tossed her head.

"It doesn't make any difference what he does anymore. I've decided to leave here anyway."

Casey waited for Mrs. Rogers to respond. When she merely nodded and sipped her tea, Casey went on.

"I can't stand it here any longer. I'm going to write Mother tonight and tell her I'm coming home."

Casey talked faster now as the excitement overcame her.

"I'll sell the barn and pay for the rest of the wire and Maude will bring a little something . . ."

Casey took a sip of her tea and watched Mrs. Rogers over the rim of the cup.

"Sorry to hear it, Casey; I'll miss you. You really plan to do it?"

Casey put her cup in its saucer, and for the first time since the thought had first occurred to her, she knew she really did mean it and relief flooded her.

"Yes, I do plan to leave. I intend to write her tonight."

Mrs. Rogers looked startled and plunged a hand into her apron pocket.

"Reminds me. I have a letter for you. That's really why I came over."

Casey took the letter and glanced at the handwriting.

"It's from Mother. Oh, thank you for bringing it over, Mrs. Rogers."

Casey put the unopened envelope on the table.

"Aren't you going to read it?" Mrs. Rogers asked.

Casey shook her head.

"Later," she said. "Mother's letters are sort of special to me and I want to read it when I'm alone."

Casey ignored the look of disappointment on Mrs. Rogers's face.

"Well, Casey, I've got to go. I hope you change your mind and stay with us."

Mrs. Rogers rose, went to the door, and paused with her hand on the knob.

"Casey, maybe if you would get out of the wire business and do something else . . ."

Casey shook her head.

"No, Mrs. Rogers. I realize now that I have only stayed this long because Texas was William's dream." She choked for a moment on her words. "And, after all, there is no more William and no more dream, is there?"

Mrs. Rogers opened the door.

"Come see me, Casey," she said, and closed the door behind her.

When the door closed, Casey let the tears roll down her cheeks.

She picked up the letter and held it to her breast for a moment, then wiped her face, opened the letter, and began to read.

My dearest Casey:

I cannot tell you of the grief that is in my heart as I bring you this news. Your father's bank has failed and this has destroyed the man. He sits all day with a bottle beside him while I try to deal with the creditors that come to the door.

I hope to be able to go to work soon, but in the meantime, if you could spare any money, it is badly needed now. Believe me, even a small amount would help.

Love,
Mother

Casey sat for a long time with the letter clutched in her hand and stared at the wall. Then she rose and took her cash from its hiding place behind the stove, counted out half of it, and put the remainder back. She opened the kitchen cabinet and looked inside. When she didn't see what she needed, she closed the cabinet and left the house.

She stumbled down the street to Rogers's store. She waited while Mrs. Rogers finished with another customer and then turned to her.

"Casey, are you all right?"

Casey nodded.

"Mrs. Rogers, I need a can of baking powder," she said.

CHAPTER 22

CASEY put half her money in the baking-powder can and wrapped it as she had before. She put the wrapped can in the cabinet, picked up her mother's letter, and read it again through a blur of tears.

"If I could just be with her," she murmured, "but I would only be a burden to her now."

It's so hot. I wish I could get a breeze through here, she thought, and moved to the open window. The early evening quiet was on the town and she could see no one moving in the street. Casey fanned herself with the edge of her skirt. Perspiration beaded on her forehead and her clothing stuck to her body.

I can't stand this, she thought. I've got to get out of here. She moved from the window, crossed the room, and went outside. She sat on the bench and tried to move the heavy air in and out of her lungs.

"I'll bet Maude is uncomfortable too," she said to herself as she rose and walked inside the barn. She waited in the semidarkness of the barn for a moment and listened to Maude's movement in her stall.

"I've never opened that back door," she told herself. "I wonder if that would help?"

She made her way the length of the barn to the big double door. She winced as she pushed upward on the heavy bar with her bruised hands. She stood the bar on end and pushed on the door until it began to move, slowly at first, then faster until it stood wide open.

"I believe I do feel a little breeze," she murmured.

She walked to the middle of the building and began to enjoy the cooling effect on her damp body as the air began to be pulled through the barn. She lifted the damp clothing away from her breast and moved it back and forth to get the cooling effect on her skin.

"My, that's better," she said aloud.

Suddenly a feeling of guilt touched her.

"I shouldn't enjoy anything with Mother in so much trouble," she told herself. "Poor Mother, poor Father. What will they do? What can I do to help?"

She looked toward the large front door outlined in the evening dusk as she walked and worried. She stopped and rested her hand on one of the stacks of wire. The air movement seemed to be stronger now and she could feel the slight pressure of the light wind against her body. I'll go in now, she thought. It should be bearable now that the air is moving.

Inside the house the stuffy heat came as a shock.

"Well, damn," she said aloud. "It's no better in here at all. I wonder why?"

She sat next to the window again and fanned herself.

"I can't stand this!" she told herself, and rose to go outside again. Outside in the dark hallway, the air flowed over her again. This barn must be like a giant chimney lying down. That's why the air moves here.

Casey pulled her clothing away from her body again.

"I think I'll sleep out here," she murmured.

She turned on her heel, went inside, and gathered her pillow and a coverlet.

"I wonder why I never noticed before that it is cooler out there?" she murmured and bent to light a lantern.

In the barn Casey carefully put the lantern to one side, piled hay in the middle of the hallway, then threw the coverlet over the hay, and dropped her pillow onto the makeshift bed. "That should do nicely," she told herself, and reached for the lantern and blew it out. Casey lay back on the mattress and let the luxury of the breeze flow over her.

"Not too bad, huh, Maude?"

Casey lay on her back with her hands under her head and breathed the fragrance that rose from the hay beneath her.

William always said we would do it in the barn sometime. For no reason the words *Poor Mother* formed in her mind and she felt the tears begin again.

When her hands began to hurt from the weight of her head, she moved them to her sides. She fought the feeling that she was somehow naked.

"Good Lord, I haven't had the thirty-eight on all day," she muttered, and rose from the straw bed.

She made her way through the darkness to her room. Inside, she struck a match and found her shotgun. "I'll feel better with this," she told herself as she loaded the weapon and carried it out to the straw bed. She slid her shotgun under the coverlet and made a place for it in the straw.

Casey lay on her side, pulled her knees up to her stomach, and tried not to think of her mother and father but their faces floated through her mind.

"I've got to help some way. I've just got to," she said into the darkness. "I've got to sell some more wire. I'll saddle Maude tomorrow if my hands will stand it and . . ."

When she woke in the darkness, all she knew for sure was that her eyes were open.

"Where am I?" she asked herself.

Her hand brushed the hardness of the shotgun under the coverlet and she remembered. Then came the sound that wasn't normal, and an uneasy feeling that there was someone else in the barn.

My God, someone's in here, she thought. She lay quietly and listened.

"I know he's in here. I know he is," she told herself.

When the sound of a voice came, its boldness was shocking.

"What the hell is it he wants done with the wire?"

"He don't care much. Scatter it or something, to scare her."

"Let's forget the wire. Let's go in her window and . . ."

"I done it once. Me and the boys done it to her once. They let me go first. He didn't say we could this time but maybe we ought to."

Casey lay rigid with fright and, in her mind, tried to match the voices with faces. The words came back to her from the night William died.

"I ain't the first. We let young Willie go first . . ." It all flashed in her mind like slides of a magic lantern and then she knew.

It is . . . It's him . . . It's the Willie that Dobson slapped down in the street, she thought.

Casey rolled quietly from her bed and fished for the weapon. When she had it in her hand, she slid into a stall next to the stacks of wire and squatted, listening.

The voice came again.

"We better scatter the wire some first. He said messing up the wire after the dog ought to be enough."

Casey listened to the sound of boot heels approaching on the dirt floor.

"Wait. Wait till they're closer," she told herself.

Casey looked through a crack in the partition and watched the shadowy forms move closer. The one on this side is Willie, I think. I remember that slouchy walk. She tried not to breathe at all as the two came closer. Her hands were sweating now, and when the men stopped directly in front of her, she felt the weapon slip in her grasp.

My God, they're right on top of me, she thought. They'll hear my heart. I know they will.

When the match flared, she was sure. This was the Willie that Dobson had downed. Without thinking she jabbed the barrel of the shotgun upward into his crotch and shouted.

"Freeze, Willie!"

The man stood frozen to the spot.

"You know who this is, Willie?"

"Is, ah, is it Mrs. Lee?"

"Yes it is, Willie. I just wanted to be sure of something."

"Yes, ma'am."

Casey watched the flame of the match burn toward Willie's fingers and took careful note of where his parner stood.

The fire of the match had dimmed and nearly gone out when Casey spoke again.

"I wanted to be sure that you knew it was me that sent you to hell without any balls," she said and pulled the trigger.

The flash of the explosion lit the barn like lightning. Blinded, Casey fired from memory at the place the other face should be. Then she scrambled as hard as she could for the front door of her barn.

CHAPTER 23

CASEY sniffed the stale tobacco odor, squeezed her eyes tight, and listened for a familiar sound.

"I have to find out some time," she told herself and opened her eyes.

Why, I'm in my own bed, she thought. She turned her head and surveyed the room. The sight of Mrs. Rogers asleep at the table with her head on her arms came as a shock.

"I wonder why she's here," she muttered and rose from the bed.

She crossed the room, put her hand on the sleeping woman's shoulder, and shook her. Mrs. Rogers jerked herself erect in the chair and Casey stepped back startled.

"Mrs. Rogers, what are you doing here?"

"Don't you know?"

"Why, no, I just woke up and there you were."

"Well, I've been looking after you since the shooting last night. I brought you in here while the men cleaned up. What happened out there, Casey?"

As the memory began to return, Casey began to shake.

"Get back in bed. Tell me later."

Casey rushed to the bed and pulled the covers up to her chin. Mrs. Rogers piled on quilts and Casey hugged the covering to herself and listened to her teeth chatter.

Suddenly she was hot again and sweat began to cover her. She threw back the covering and sat on the side of the bed

"Did you say, 'since last night'?"

"Yes, since we found you about midnight. You've been having those chills off and on ever since."

Casey sat silent for a moment.

"Mrs. Rogers, I, ah, I shot at a prowler out there last night. Did I hit him?"

Casey flinched under the woman's unbelieving stare.

"Casey, don't give me that! We found two dead men out there. One had half his head shot away and the other had no ass at all. You had to be close to do that. You know damn well you hit them!"

Casey tried to make her voice sound weak.

"Well, I did think maybe . . ."

Mrs. Rogers's voice was firm now.

"Casey, come off it. We found you passed out in the front door with that crazy shotgun under you and both barrels had been fired."

The woman took out her tobacco, began to roll a cigarette, squinted one eye, and stared.

"I guess you know that fool sheriff will want to talk to you. He said for me to notify him as soon as you came to yourself."

Casey sighed and crossed the room to the water bucket.

"I suppose Billings will make a big thing out of it. I dread facing him."

She took a dipper of water from the bucket and drank. She put the dipper back in the bucket and kept her back toward Mrs. Rogers as she spoke again.

"Mrs. Rogers, has Red . . . has Mr. McCaslin been around?"

"He stayed around for awhile but he rode out a little after noon looking mad and mean."

Casey nodded, crossed the room, and seated herself on the bed again.

"Did you say Mr. Billings was here?"

"Casey, everyone in town has been here at one time or another. Yes, he was here and said he would be back."

"I can't stand that man, Mrs. Rogers. Will you stay with me while he's here?"

"Oh, I think he means well, Casey. He's just ignorant."

Casey shuddered at the thought of having to deal with the fat man again. She lay back on the bed and closed her eyes.

"If I could just sleep for a long time . . ."

She lay quietly and courted oblivion.

Mrs. Rogers's voice sliced through her comfort.

"Casey, he is coming down the street."

Casey felt her heart jump and she put her hand on her breast.

"Red?" she asked.

"No, Casey, it's Sheriff Billings."

Casey felt the color rise in her face.

"Tell him I'm sick," she said.

"Nope. Might as well get it over with. The law requires him to investigate a death."

Casey pulled the covers up to her chin.

"You stay right here, then. I don't want to be alone with that man."

"I'll stay, Casey."

Casey closed her eyes and waited for the knock on the door. I hope this doesn't take long, she thought.

When it came, the knock was somehow softer than she had expected and Casey felt a little flow of confidence.

"I can handle him," she told herself. "With Mrs. Rogers here."

She smelled the man before she heard his voice.

"I have business with Casey, Mrs. Rogers."

The coldness in Mrs. Rogers's voice startled her and Casey opened her eyes.

"Casey?"

"Er, ah, Mrs. Lee, I mean."

"Come in, then, Mr. Billings."

Casey felt the sweat begin to spread over her body again

and she wished she could remove the covering. I should have dressed, she thought. I feel so naked in this nightgown.

"I hope this won't take very long, Mr. Billings. Mrs. Lee is not feeling at all well."

"I'll try, Mrs. Rogers. Duty, you know, duty."

Casey didn't speak until the man had seated himself.

"Hello, Sheriff," she said.

"Well, young woman, you do seem to have your problems."

"Yes."

"Tell me about it."

Casey turned her head so that she couldn't see the patches of sweat under the man's arms.

"There's really not much to tell. I was sleeping in the barn and . . ."

"Sleeping in the barn?"

"Yes, it was hot and there was a breeze out there, so I piled up some hay and slept on it."

"Strange place to sleep."

Casey ignored the comment.

"As I said, I was asleep and something woke me."

"What? What was it that woke you up?"

"I'm not sure. I felt a presence, I suppose."

"A what?"

"A presence. I could feel that someone else was in the barn."

"Never heard of such a thing."

Casey let the exasperation show in her voice.

"I don't know, Sheriff. I just woke up, that's all."

Casey moved back on the bed as the fat man leaned toward her. She felt the trembling beginning inside and she struggled for control.

"I waited and listened. Suddenly two men were talking about what to do to my wire." She hesitated. "Or to me," she said.

She tried not to retch as Billings's face moved even closer and his tongue moved over his upper lip.

"Did they? Did they do like them men done before, or anything?"

"No, Sheriff, they did not. They only talked about it."

"Are you sure they didn't do nothing like that? They didn't touch your, ah, body or nothing?"

She could hear the excitement in his voice and she wished she could hide her head.

"No, Sheriff. I hid in one of the stalls and . . ."

"You trapped them?"

Casey sighed. I can't tell this fool everything that happened, she thought. She pulled the covering around her and sat up suddenly in the bed.

"Sheriff Billings. Here it is in a nutshell. I hid in a stall, and when they started to steal my wire, I shot at them. Is that clear?"

Casey let herself enjoy the look of disappointment on his face.

"That's all. That's the way it was," she said.

The cold sound of Mrs. Rogers's voice cut across the room.

"She needs to rest now, Mr. Billings."

Casey looked quickly at the woman and then at Billings. Billings sat silent for a moment and then looked up at Mrs. Rogers. When Mrs. Rogers made a small movement with her head, he picked up his hat and started for the door.

Why, she ordered him out of here! Casey marveled.

When he was halfway across the room, Mrs. Rogers put a hand on his chest and stopped him.

"There will be no need for you to come back now, will there, Mr. Billings?"

"Well now, Mrs. Rogers, I might need . . ."

Casey tried to shrink herself as the man glanced quickly toward her. Then Mrs. Rogers's voice chilled the room again.

"You have your report. Two prowlers tried to steal her wire and she shot at them."

Casey watched Billings closely while the man ducked his head and looked at the floor.

"Yes, ma'am," he said, and went out the door.

Casey threw off the covering, pulled her gown down to her feet, and hugged her knees while the older woman closed the door and then went to the window and looked out.

"She's watching to see that he really leaves," Casey told herself. Then she spoke to Mrs. Rogers.

"Good for you! Do you think he'll really stay away now?"

"He'll stay away. He doesn't have credit with anyone else. How about some tea?"

Casey swung her legs around and sat on the edge of the bed while Mrs. Rogers set out the tea things. When the tea was ready, Casey accepted the cup.

"Thank you, Mrs. Rogers. You're so good to me."

Casey sipped the tea while Mrs. Rogers pulled her chair close to the bed and then leaned back and rolled a cigarette. She lit the cigarette and pulled the smoke deep into her lungs before she spoke.

"Casey, when you feel able, I'd like for you to tell me everything that happened out there in the barn, but it can wait."

Casey nodded.

"I can tell you one thing, Mrs. Rogers. I'm sure now who killed my dog."

When the woman didn't respond, Casey said no more. Mrs. Rogers turned her head and stared out the window into the distance; then she spoke softly, "Casey?"

"Yes, Mrs. Rogers?"

"There's something I have to know."

Puzzled, Casey watched the woman's face turn pink.

"Casey, you and McCaslin. You did go to bed with him, didn't you?"

Casey spoke barely above a whisper, "Yes."

She waited and watched the woman squirm for a moment before she spoke again.

"Casey, was it good? Really good like all these women around here say it would . . ."

Casey gasped.

"Why, Mrs. Rogers!" she said.

CHAPTER 24

CASEY moved around her room straightening things and trying to keep her mind off Red McCaslin. She opened the kitchen cabinet and scanned the contents. Her eye fell on the baking-powder can in its brown wrapping.

"Oh, Lord! I forgot about poor Mother," she said and took the can from the shelf. I'll get this off today. It's been two days since he rode out. I wonder where he went? She smiled at the picture that came into her mind. I did tell him to stay away. Maybe I scared him with the shotgun.

She flexed the fingers of her right hand and winced at the pain that remained. Then she strapped on the .38, took the can, and stepped out the door into the sun-baked street. She glanced toward the blacksmith shop. Buck is busy today, she thought, as she noted the horses tied at the rail. That one seems familiar; I wonder if I know him.

Worry about her parents closed in on her again as she walked, and she tightened her grip on the can.

"I've got to find a way to help," she told herself. "I'll get on that horse and call on every farm and ranch around here if I have to. I'll talk some of them into buying that wire if it's the last thing I ever do."

Inside the store she presented her package for mailing and Mrs. Rogers tossed it into the mail sack.

"Well, the fat's in the fire now, Casey."

"What has happened?"

"Trouble, that's what. Trouble between McCaslin and Anthony."

Casey clutched at her breast.

"Did they fight? Is Red all right? I mean, was anyone hurt?"

"No, they didn't fight. They say Red quit his job with the association and that Anthony is looking for a gun to replace him."

Casey clamped her lips together and tried to keep her toes from curling in her boots.

"A gun? A gun? Is that all Red is? Just a gun?"

Casey forced her toes to straighten and waited for the woman to answer.

"No, Casey, not Red. He made that clear from the beginning. He told the association that he would use his gun if he needed to but they couldn't tell him where to aim it."

Her toes began to relax and Casey wiggled them in the boots.

"Is that what the trouble with Anthony was about?"

Mrs. Rogers leaned over the counter and beckoned to Casey. Casey leaned closer and strained to hear as the woman whispered.

"Anthony's cook told me she heard it all. Anthony wanted to point Red's gun at Grimley. The cook said Anthony told Red to pull the trigger if he had to."

Casey gasped.

"Grimley! Why he's the nicest . . ."

Mrs. Rogers held up her hand and spoke in a normal tone.

"True, but he has made the mistake of getting in Anthony's way. He'll get you, too, before he's through."

"Me. Why me? Just because I sell the wire?"

Casey's heart pounded as she spoke and she studied Mrs. Rogers's face and waited for an answer.

"That's part of it but there's more. Anthony doesn't want the boundary between him and Grimley fenced but that doesn't make too much difference just now. Not as long as his cattle can go around the end of Grimley's wire across your place to water."

Casey nodded and stared into space.

"That's what Grimley meant," she said.

"What do you mean, Casey? What did Grimley say to you?"

Casey stood silently at the counter slowly nodding her head as she recalled Grimley's remark.

"Casey! What did Grimley say?"

Casey brought her attention back to the conversation.

"He just . . . well, he didn't say much but he did ask me if Anthony had ever offered to buy my place. When I said no, Grimley seemed to think that was strange. He said he would have if he were Anthony."

Little tingles of fear began in her body as Casey asked the next question: "If my little place is important to Anthony, why would he want to harm me? I would think he would want to be friendly with me."

Mrs. Rogers leaned over the counter again.

"Well, Casey, here's the way I see it. Anthony is a proud man and he doesn't want to have to ask anybody for anything. If he could run you out of here soon enough . . ."

Casey turned back to the counter.

"Soon enough for what?"

"Before you fence your place. Everybody knows that you will have to fence your place soon to show that you have faith in the wire."

Casey stared at the woman in amazement.

"My God, Mrs. Rogers, I hadn't even thought of it. I couldn't afford the wire and labor even at my cost. Is it me that's stupid, or is it Anthony?"

Casey leaned against the counter, tapped her foot, and worried while Mrs. Rogers attended to a customer. When the woman returned, Casey ignored her presence and let the frightening thoughts play in her mind.

Mrs. Rogers waved her hand before Casey's face and snapped her fingers.

"Casey, Casey, are you with me?"

Casey looked at Mrs. Rogers.

"Mrs. Rogers, what if Anthony had offered to buy our

place from William and what if William had refused him? We know Willie worked for Anthony and I know that Willie was there that night . . ."

Casey's heart pounded as the older woman's face paled and threw both hands to her face.

"Oh, my God, Casey! Oh, my God!"

Stunned, Casey felt no further need for conversation and she could see that Mrs. Rogers had nothing more to say either. Casey turned to leave.

"If you hear anything you think I need to know . . ." she said and went out the door on to the board sidewalk.

Casey walked slowly toward her barn. She could feel the sun on her back but there was a chill inside of her. She walked with her head down in thought.

I wonder what Red will do? I wonder if he will move on? I may never see him again if he does that. I'm in real trouble. What should I do next?

Her mother's words came into her mind again: "Casey, one can only live a day at a time. Dwell not on yesterday nor tomorrow. One must do one's best."

Casey stopped in the street and let the sun beat down upon her back.

"I'll do that. I'll live just one day at a time. Right now I have to figure out how to sell wire."

Casey stopped at the entrance of the barn.

"I have hardly looked at Maude lately. If I'm going to start riding her, I'd better have Buck see to her shoes," she told herself.

Casey walked the length of the long, cool stable and stopped at Maude's stall. She moved in next to the animal and patted her neck.

"Ready for some exercise, girl? Don't roll that eye at me, Maude. Lately you've done nothing but loaf around. You come with me."

Casey untied the halter rope, pushed against Maude's chest, and backed her out of the stall. She led the animal out of the barn and over to the blacksmith shop. She tied

Maude next to the big red stallion and went inside.

She waited till Buck stopped his pounding and looked up at her.

"Buck, I've got Maude tied outside. I'm going to start riding her hard and I'd like for you to check her over for me. Check her shoes and, well, you know horses. Just let me know if you think she is healthy and everything."

Buck nodded.

"Soon as I finish this," he said.

Casey turned to leave, then turned back.

"Buck, who owns that big red horse out there? He looks familiar to me."

Buck picked up his hammer.

"Some stranger," he said. "Left him here this morning. He's been traveling some, though; I can tell you that. His shoes was plumb wore out."

Outside Casey paused a moment and looked at Maude beside the red horse. The animals stood quietly and Maude moved her head from time to time to touch her nose against the stallion's. When Maude stared back at her and slowly closed one eye, Casey smiled.

"Hussy!" she said and looked toward her barn.

"Why that's Mrs. Rogers on the bench," she told herself and hurried to the woman's side.

"Come inside, Mrs. Rogers. I'll fix us something."

"No, I don't have time. I just wanted to let you know . . ."

Casey froze.

"Let me know what?"

"Well, Mr. Rogers came in awhile ago. He says the talk down at the saloon is that Anthony has already hired somebody to replace McCaslin."

Casey sank to the bench beside Mrs. Rogers.

"Who? Who is it? Is it somebody from around here? Do you think he will have him kill Grimley?"

"Nobody knows him. Not yet, anyway. They say he is as fast as he can be. Rogers says the man is a gambler out of New Orleans by way of Waco."

CHAPTER 25

CASEY sat by the lamp and read the paper again. I wonder why I didn't read this when Mr. Dobson first gave it to me, she thought. It was right there with the invoice. She moved the paper closer to the light and read the circular again:

> There is hardly anyone who uses four-point wire, as they have found by experience that two-point Glidden wire turns all stock, looks better, and is not so liable to breakage. There is also a little more length to the pound. We can furnish four-point wire if our customers insist on having it. The hog wire has barbs about three inches apart; cattle wire, about six inches apart. Price is liable to advance or decline any day, so we cannot quote a price for the season.

Casey dropped her hand that held the paper into her lap and thought about what she had read.

Good Lord! I didn't even know there was such a thing as four-point wire. I'll never be able to talk anybody into buying this stuff. I don't know anything about wire or posts or fences, or anything else, for that matter.

She put the paper to one side and sat for a long time and thought again about what she had read. Suddenly she smiled.

"That Mr. Glidden is a smart man," she told herself. "He couldn't care less whether people buy two-point or four-point wire. He just wants them to buy wire. If he can get them to decide which, they have already made a decision to use the wire."

Casey reached for paper and a pen and began to write.

Dear Mr. Glidden:

I need five hundred of the little circulars you sent me with the invoice for the wire. It is my intention to distribute as many of these as possible in this community. I hope to start a controversy about which wire is better, two-point or four-point. It seems to me that it would be much better for our customers to argue about that than to argue about whether to use the wire at all.

Sincerely,
C. Lee

Casey put the letter in an envelope, addressed it, and laid the letter aside. She glanced at the clock on the wall. I'm really not sleepy, she thought, but what else is there to do at eight-thirty?

She rose and had begun to undress for bed when the knock sounded. I'll bet that's Mrs. Rogers, she thought. Maybe she's learned something more.

"Just a moment," she called and hurried back into her clothes.

Casey swung the door wide.

"Come in, Mrs. Rogers." Then she gasped, "Judson Wingate, where'd you come from?"

Casey stepped back from the door and tried to regain her composure.

"Come in, Mr. Wingate. How nice to see you again."

She waited while the man came through the door, stopped just inside, removed his hat, and looked around.

"You live here now?"

"I've lived here for some time," Casey said. "Won't you have a seat?"

"I rode past your old place on the way in. When I found it empty, I was afraid you had left the country."

Casey smiled.

"No. I'm still here and I guess I'll have to stay as long as I can survive. Now tell me all about yourself."

"He looks tired and drawn," she told herself.

"Have you been well, Jud?"

"Well enough, I suppose. I've moved around quite a bit and pretty fast. One town after another, one poker game after another. I'm pretty tired of running . . ."

Casey looked at him and remembered the note she had snatched from the floor of the barn loft. As though he read her thoughts, he suddenly asked, "Did you find my note?"

Casey felt the flush in her face.

"Yes, Jud, I found it."

"Well, Casey, the longer I rode, the more I knew that part of what I had written in the note was not true. The part about never seeing you again. As time went on, I knew I just didn't want to live if I could never see you again."

Casey sat quietly and let her heart pound. I've got to change the subject, she thought.

"Jud, are you still running?"

She watched the sober expression cross his face.

"Not exactly," he said. "I got word that the man in Waco didn't die, so there's no hue and cry after me anyway."

Casey leaned forward and strained to hear as the man looked away from her, dropped his gaze to the floor, and spoke softly.

"Everything since then has been judged a fair fight."

"Fair fight? You mean there have been more?"

Casey studied him and waited for his answer.

"Some," he said. "But let's not talk about that. Let's talk about you and me."

She tried to make her voice soft.

"Jud, there is no 'you and me.'"

"You said you found my note."

Casey nodded. "I did find it, Jud. But I must tell you

that I did not develop any of the feelings for you that you expressed to me in that note."

She reached and put her hand lightly on his arm.

"And, Jud, the note said you would never be back."

Casey fought to push back an uneasy, frightened feeling.

"He's a stranger now," she told herself. "It's hard to believe I ever needed him so."

His voice broke into her thoughts.

"When I wrote the note, I knew it was too soon for you. It seemed to be the only decent thing to do. It had been a long time since I had done anything decent . . ."

Casey broke in.

"Jud. Mr. Wingate, I . . ."

When Wingate held up a hand, Casey looked at the slender fingers. He has such graceful hands, she thought, and then heard his words again.

"I don't mean to rush you, Casey. I think in time you will realize that more happened between us than you thought possible. I know that it did for me and I know for a fact that I cannot, I will not, try to live the rest of my life without you."

Casey heard her words tumbling one after another and she wished that she didn't have to say them.

"Jud, I have no such feelings. I don't want to hurt you in any way but I don't even have time to think of such a thing. I have serious problems here and . . ."

The knock on the door brought a flood of relief and Casey hurried to answer it. When Casey opened the door, Mrs. Rogers stepped inside. She looked at Wingate and turned to leave without speaking. Casey put her hand on Mrs. Rogers's arm to stop her.

"Mrs. Rogers, this is Mr. Judson Wingate. Mr. Wingate, this is my good friend, Mrs. Rogers."

Casey looked from one to the other as Mrs. Rogers nodded but did not speak. Wingate nodded, then picked up his hat.

"I'll be leaving now, Casey," he said. "I'll be busy tomorrow but I'll be back as soon as possible. Nice to meet you, Mrs. Rogers."

Casey closed the door behind Wingate, turned back to Mrs. Rogers, and stared in amazement. The woman's mouth moved but no sound came out. She jabbed at the air with a forefinger and silently moved her mouth.

"Mrs. Rogers! Are you all right?"

Casey listened as the sound returned to the woman's voice and she continued to jab the air with her finger.

"That's, that's, that's him, Casey!"

"Who?"

"Him. That fellow is McCaslin's replacement. That's what I came to tell you. I just found out his name."

Casey sank into a chair, put her hands over her face, and rocked back and forth. After a while she uncovered her face.

"Mrs. Rogers, that's the man who found me and took care of me. He taught me to use the thirty-eight."

"Not very well, he didn't."

Casey ignored the remark.

"He seems so different now. It's almost like he's not the same person."

Mrs. Rogers struggled to her feet.

"He may not be, Casey. They say he has killed twelve men, half of them in the past six months. I've got to go. I'm sorry about your friend."

***

Casey lay on her bed and stared into the darkness. He *is* different now, she thought, but I can't quite decide just how. There is a kind of danger about him now that I didn't feel before. Or is it just because of what Mrs. Rogers said? I don't see how he could possibly think that I would just fall into his arms. I never gave him any reason to . . . such a thing would be impossible . . . I could never . . .

She turned on her side in the dark and hugged her knees. The image of Jud's slender hands and long fingers floated in her mind.

"Not at all like William's," she murmured.

CHAPTER 26

CASEY smoothed Maude's saddle blanket, then grunted as she heaved the heavy saddle onto the animal's back. She tightened the girth, backed Maude out of the stall, and led her to the front of the building. Outside she tied the animal to the pen that had held the Stanton bull and left her standing while she went into the living quarters.

She put sandwiches into a flour sack, strapped on the .38, picked up the shotgun, and went outside. She lifted the flap of the saddlebag and put the sandwiches in. She checked the shotgun to be sure it was not loaded and tried to stuff it in beside the sandwiches.

"Well, it's not going to ride there," she grumbled and looked for a place to tie the weapon to the saddle.

I believe I can tie it behind, she thought, and reached up to fasten the gun in place. As she worked with the whang strings, her eyes fell on the toenail scratches on the saddle skirt.

"Poor Stranger," she murmured, "how she did love to ride back here."

Casey put her foot in the stirrup, swung into the saddle, rode into the street, and tried to decide where to go first. She leaned in the saddle and peered into the blacksmith shop. "*Hmmmm*. Buck's late this morning."

I think I'll ride out to Grimley's first. He may be able to suggest someone that I should call on. She turned Maude and rode down the street and out of town. When she had worked Maude into her one good gait, Casey began to enjoy the early-morning ride.

There *is* something about this country, she thought. I know how William felt about it all. Strange, I really didn't understand his feelings about Texas while he was alive. She smiled. It was just so wonderful to be with him that I really didn't care where I was. She rode and enjoyed the feel of the memory of how it had been to be with William; then she smiled again.

"I was such a ninny, it's a wonder he could stand me at all," she said aloud.

Casey stood in the stirrups and pulled her damp clothing away from her buttocks, then sat back and hooked one leg over the saddle horn.

"There, that's better," she told herself, and then, with a shock, she noticed the lone rider off to her left.

He's about a quarter of a mile away, she thought. I wonder if he knows I'm here? She put her right foot back in its stirrup and tried not to breathe too hard. She touched Maude gently with her heels and stared at the horseman.

Casey tried to ignore the tingle of fear that began when the lone rider began to move too. She let Maude walk and tried to force herself to look straight ahead. When she had ridden a way, she glanced quickly to the left.

"He's still there, Maude."

She kicked Maude into a trot for a few minutes, then shot a quick glance to the left again. She could not control a quick intake of breath as she saw that the rider's animal also moved at a trot.

Well, at least he hasn't gotten any closer to me, she thought. Probably doesn't even know I'm here. I wonder why he doesn't use the road like everybody else.

Casey looked quickly at the sun.

"Nearly noon," she said aloud, "I'll stop and eat soon."

She let Maude plod along at her own pace and looked from time to time at the lone rider. I'm beginning to get used to him, she thought. He's probably all right.

When the rider disappeared behind a small hill, Casey pulled Maude up sharply. "I'll eat now and maybe he'll be gone by the time I have finished," she told herself. She turned her animal off the road and dismounted. She fished the sandwiches out of the saddlebag and ate standing beside her mare. When she had finished the sandwiches, Casey drank from the canteen, stuffed the flour sack into the saddlebag, and swung back into the saddle.

I won't look for the rider, she thought and faced herself forward and stared down the road. She sat on her horse for a moment then.

"I've got to know," she muttered and turned her head to the left. When she saw the lone figure on top of the hill standing perfectly still, the fear began again.

"Oh, God! He waited. He is after me," she groaned.

Casey drew the .38 from its holster and checked to be sure it was loaded. Then she reached behind the saddle and untied the shotgun and broke it open. She twisted herself till she could reach the saddlebag, then found shells for the gun and listened to the hollow sound as they went into the chambers. She decided to ride with the shotgun resting on the saddle horn.

Casey rode and tried to fight the fear.

"I must be getting close to Grimley's now," she told herself, and glanced again at the rider.

When she finally saw the Grimley house in the distance, she kicked Maude into a lope. She looked again at the rider and fear filled her completely. His horse is matching Maude stride for stride, she thought. What can he want with me?

As she neared the Grimley house, Casey slowed Maude to a walk and rode into the yard.

"Oh, Maude, how nice! He's fenced her garden."

When no one approached, she remembered what William had told her: "In Texas you never dismount until you're invited."

Casey turned and looked for the rider again.

"He's not as close now," she muttered. "But I can see him. He's still out there, just standing, watching me."

She jumped at the sound of the door and the woman's voice.

"Get down, get down. You rode in so quiet, I didn't know you was there. Excuse my manners. Come in and set."

Casey dismounted, stuffed the shotgun into the saddlebag, and tied Maude to the lonesome mesquite tree in the middle of the yard.

"I'm Casey Lee," she said, and extended her hand.

The older woman took her hand and gave it a slight shake.

She has calluses like a man, Casey thought.

"Come on in. I knowed who you was. I seen you in town. Mrs. Rogers pointed you out. I would of guessed, anyway. You're the only woman around here that carries a gun."

Casey followed the woman through the door. Inside she motioned Casey toward a large table and waited until Casey had seated herself. Then, without speaking, the woman poured two glasses of buttermilk and put out a plate of cold cornbread. Then she seated herself across from Casey.

"What brings you out our way, Mrs. Lee?"

Casey sipped the buttermilk.

"I rode out to see if Mr. Grimley was getting along all right with the wire and to see if he might know of anyone who would be in need of wire themselves."

Casey waited while the woman drained her glass, put it on the table, and stared at her.

"Have you been saved, Mrs. Lee?"

Casey felt the color rise to her face.

"Well, yes, I think so, Mrs. Grimley. I'm not a great churchgoer, but I think . . ."

"If you was saved, you would know about it. Let us pray."

Casey stared as Mrs. Grimley placed her elbows on the table, clasped her hands, and looked toward the ceiling.

"Lord, we come to you in earnest prayer. We have here this woman that in her heart wants to be saved. They is some that thinks of her as a loose woman but, Lord, it stands to reason that some of it ain't her fault. Lord, this woman needs savin' and we are askin' for that. Amen."

The prayer was over before Casey could bow her head and she sat stunned for a moment.

"Amen," Casey said.

The woman lowered her head.

"Now, honey, just don't sin no more and everything will be all right. Grimley will be back here in a little while. He likes the wire. It's me that made him do it. When I seen that wire, I told him, 'Grimley, you get that wire and you fence my garden.'"

Casey shifted in the chair and said nothing.

My God, the woman's mad, she thought. Then she felt the rough hand touch her bare arm as the voice began again.

"This country is hard on a woman, Mrs. Lee. Some of 'em go crazy. Maggie Miller done it. She went plumb crazy. It's the wind, the everlastin' wind, that does it to 'em. That and fightin' them goddam animals out of their gardens all the time. I know that's what done it to Maggie. I said to Grimley, 'You get me that wire,' I said to him."

Casey rose.

"I really must go. Thank you very much, Mrs. Grimley." The woman followed Casey to the door.

"Nice of you to ride all the way out here. I enjoyed our visit. I don't get to listen to another woman talk very often."

Mrs. Grimley followed Casey across the yard and waited while she untied Maude.

"Here comes Grimley now," she said.

Casey waited while he approached.

"I'm glad I didn't miss you, Mr. Grimley. I rode out to

see how you are getting along with the wire and to ask if
you know anyone who might be interested in buying
some."

"Well, there have been some that have come and looked.
Some seemed to like the idea and some was against it."

The man smiled.

"I happen to know that some of them that was against it
don't have no cash," he said.

Casey took a deep breath.

"Mr. Grimley, have you had any trouble about the wire?
With Anthony or anybody? I mean the way Anthony acted
in town that day . . ."

"Well, not much, really. Anthony did send McCaslin to
talk to me about it but I just sent him on his way."

He looked sharply at Casey.

"I heard about your trouble. Sorry you had to go
through that. Good riddance, though. Them two."

Casey threw the reins over Maude's neck and mounted
the saddle.

"Thank you, Mr. Grimley. You don't think of anyone I
should call on, then?"

Casey waited while the man slowly shook his head.

"I don't think that's the way to do it, ma'am."

"Oh?"

"No, ma'am, seems to me like it would be better to stay
close by in case somebody come lookin' to buy wire. Everybody is situated too far apart for you to ride all over the
country trying to find them."

He turned and glanced at the sun.

"It'll be dark by the time you get home now."

Casey leaned on the saddle horn.

"You may be right," she said. "I hadn't thought about it
that way. About all that riding, I mean."

Casey turned toward Mrs. Grimley.

"Thank you for your hospitality, Mrs. Grimley. I enjoyed the buttermilk."

When the woman didn't answer but turned and scurried

toward the house, Casey turned a questioning look toward Grimley.

"Did she pray for you, Mrs. Lee?"

Casey nodded and watched the man's eyes fill with tears.

"Don't mind her, ma'am. She's had it hard."

Grimley looked away from Casey and into the distance and spoke as though to himself.

"Sometimes I think it's the wind," he said.

Casey followed Grimley's gaze until she saw the lone horseman again.

"Do you know who that person is, Mr. Grimley?"

She waited while Grimley squinted at the rider.

"I'm not sure, but if I was going to guess, I'd say that was Anthony's new man," he said.

***

Casey gripped the shotgun and kept an urging heel in Maude's side. The rider, to the right now, on the return to town, kept pace with her.

"He's almost stride for stride with me again," Casey told herself. "I believe that *is* Jud Wingate."

I've got to let Maude slow up some, she thought, and brought the animal to a walk. She faced the setting sun and tried to fight back the fear.

He hasn't really done anything, so if it isn't Jud, maybe I don't really have anything to be afraid of. He has to be interested in me, though, or he would never have made the ride back to town.

As the remaining crescent of a sun sank in the west, Casey spurred Maude into a lope again. She wished that the town would come into view. She looked from side to side and gripped the shotgun tighter as the night began to wrap itself around her. When she saw the lights of town in the distance, she spurred Maude on. A rhythm clicked in her mind. It's Jud. It's Jud. I know it's Jud out here looking after me.

CHAPTER 27

CASEY stopped Maude at Buck's watering trough and let her drink. She looked over her shoulder at the direction from which she had come.

"No sign of him now," she told herself; then she looked toward her barn. It sure looks dark in there, she thought. She broke open the shotgun again and made sure it was loaded. She snapped it shut and reached for the comfort of the .38.

When Maude lifted her head from the trough, Casey rode her to the barn. She tied the animal to the bull pen, went inside, put the shotgun on the table, and lit the lantern. She carried the lantern outside, led Maude into the barn, removed the heavy saddle, and tied her up in the stall.

She patted the animal on her neck, then propped open the heavy lid of the oats bin. Casey leaned in and felt in the darkness for the bucket.

This is running low, she thought as she scraped the corners. She poured the oats into Maude's feeding trough and pitched the bucket back into the bin; then something she had heard at Buck's floated into her mind and she could hear the cowboy's voice.

"Feed? Oh, I give him a gallon a day, and if I ride him after midnight, I give him a little more."

"Well, it's not midnight yet, but I did ride her hard. I'll give her a little more," she muttered.

Casey leaned as far into the bin as she could and felt in the darkness for more. The edge of the bin cut into her stomach and she struggled to keep her balance while stretching to reach the far corners of the container.

"Casey! Casey!"

Casey dropped the bucket at the sound of the hoarse whisper, and her feet left the ground. The edge of the bin pressed harder against her stomach and she pushed against the bottom of the bin with the tips of her fingers in an effort to regain her balance.

Casey swore to herself.

"Damn him! Goddamn him. I don't hear from him for days. He's never around when I need him; then he comes sneaking up behind me when I'm upside down with my butt in the air."

"Red McCaslin, you get me out of here!" she growled.

Casey felt the strong hands caress her buttocks as they pushed her feet toward the ground.

With her feet set solidly, Casey jerked her body erect and spun to face the man. She pushed hard against his chest as his arms closed around her and the passion began to rise in her.

She pushed and turned her head one way, then another; then she stopped her struggle. She clung to him for a moment and pressed her face against his chest.

Ruffles? Ruffles? she thought. Red doesn't wear a ruffled shirt.

She pulled herself away again.

"Jud Wingate, you turn me loose!"

Casey let the passion build higher as he held her closer for a moment.

"Put me down, Jud!"

Then, as she felt the softness of hay against her back, she drew him to her and returned his kisses.

***

Casey stomped up and down her room and talked to herself.

"You did it! You did it again! Judson Wingate touched

you and you melted in his arms. You melted and the man never said over three words. All he ever said was, 'Goodnight, my darling.'"

Casey picked up her clothing from the floor and idly brushed straw from the garments. Then she heated water and poured it into the wash pan. She stripped off her gown and bathed herself carefuly.

As she dressed, Casey worried. I can't do that! What kind of woman am I? If I don't take myself in hand, I'll be carrying somebody's bastard and I won't even know whose it is.

Casey picked up her brush and turned to the mirror again.

"Wipe that silly grin off your face," she said to the reflection. "You'll never love anyone but William." She rested the brush on the chest and frowned at the reflection.

"Are you lying to me again?" she asked.

The sound of a wagon outside her door interrupted and Casey went outside and approached the woman who drove it.

"Good morning. What can I do for you?"

"My man said I could ask about some wire for my garden. How much is it?"

"It's two dollars a roll."

Casey watched the look of disappointment cross the woman's face and she quickly spoke again.

"That's the regular price but I have a special price on small amounts for gardens."

She watched the woman's face change again and she listened to herself expand a thought that she had never known existed.

"Yes, on small amounts for women who want to protect their gardens, the price is one-fifty or one dollar and another dollar's worth of trade goods, eggs, or whatever. Right now I could use a few bushels of oats."

Casey felt good when the woman smiled.

"I've got two dollars now if you'd trust me for the oats. I need two rolls of the wire."

Casey held out her hand for the money.

"I'll trust you for the oats," she said. "Pull your wagon into the barn."

Inside, Casey lugged one of the rolls to the wagon and the other woman handled the other roll. When she had dropped her burden in the wagon box, the woman climbed to the driver's seat.

"Why is she frowning?" Casey asked herself. "She seemed pleased a moment ago."

"Thank you for the business," Casey said.

Casey waited for some reply as the woman's frown deepened and she leaned from the driver's seat.

"This wasn't no special deal just for me, was it? My man won't take no charity."

Casey laughed.

"Oh no! That's my standard deal for garden wire. Limit five rolls."

Casey backed away from the wheel as the horses shifted and moved the wagon a little.

"In fact, I'd appreciate it if you would tell your friends about my special price."

The woman nodded, tightened the reins, and started to back the team. Then she stopped.

"I'll bring your oats tomorrow."

"You don't have to be in such a hurry," Casey said.

"It's Saturday. We was coming in anyway," the woman said, and backed her wagon out of the barn.

Casey took the two dollars inside and put it in her hiding place.

I think I'll go visit Mrs. Rogers, she thought. Maybe she's heard something about Red. She stepped out the door and turned back to be sure it latched properly.

"Seems you're doing quite a business this morning."

She looked over her shoulder at the man sitting on the bench. She waited while the man finished rolling a cigarette, ran his tongue down its length, examined it carefully, and then put it in his mouth.

Casey felt the blood pounding in her ears.

He's a devil, she thought. He just shows up here sitting on my bench rolling a cigarette. She tossed her head. And I haven't seen him in days.

"Yes, Red. I sell a little wire now and then."

"He's not going to fluster me this time," she told herself, and seated herself on the bench beside him.

"Five hundred and two," he said, and lit the cigarette.

Casey shook her head.

"What? Five hundred and two what?"

"You have sold exactly five hundred and two rolls of wire, to date."

"Oh, that. Well, I have hope. Did you come here to argue with me about the wire again? I've been worried. I was afraid maybe you'd left for good. I mean, nobody seemed to know where, or, well . . ."

Casey watched Red McCaslin destroy the butt of the cigarette with his thick fingers, then mash it into the ground.

"Nope, I'm not going to leave. I have other plans. I guess you heard I quit my job with the association. Yep, Casey, I'm going to stay right here."

"What do you plan to do then, Red?"

Casey felt his eyes like a physical force as he looked directly at her.

"I'm going to marry a widow and straighten her out some."

Casey rose and he rose with her.

"Well, good luck with the widow, Mr. McCaslin."

She turned away, then felt his strong grip on her arm as he spun her to face him again.

"Who in hell is Judson Wingate and what is he to you?" he demanded.

Casey let the anger flare.

"He is a man that does some things a helluva lot better than you do," she snapped, then jerked her arm free and stormed toward Rogers's store.

CHAPTER 28

"HI, Casey, heard you sold some wire this morning. How was your ride out to Grimley's?"

Casey sighed.

"Mrs. Rogers, is there anything at all that I do that you don't know about immediately?"

As she asked the question, the experience last night with Jud in the barn went through her mind, and Casey knew the color was rising in her face. She felt the blush deepen as Mrs. Rogers spoke.

"I doubt if I know it *all*, Casey," she said.

Casey opened the catalogue on the counter before her and flipped the pages.

"I sold some wire to a woman this morning for her garden, that's all."

"Sloppy business."

"What do you mean, Mrs. Rogers?"

"You sold merchandise on credit and you didn't even ask the woman's name."

Casey stamped her foot.

"Now, dammit, how do you know that? You do know everything!"

"Relax, Casey. You're too grumpy this morning. That was Mrs. Johnson. She asked me to tell you who she is. She said you didn't ask. They're poor as church mice but she'll bring your oats tomorrow. Have you seen McCaslin?"

Casey turned her back to the woman, leaned against the counter, and crossed her arms.

"Yes, I just saw him."

"How about your friend Wingate?"

Casey fought the feeling of guilt.

"I saw him a few minutes last night."

"I heard he was in town all day yesterday. Spent the day playing poker. That's what Mr. Rogers said. God knows, that man should know. He's spending all day every day in that saloon now."

Casey felt the weakness flow through her and she gripped the edge of the counter behind her.

"It wasn't him! It wasn't Jud out there looking after me at all!" she told herself.

"Played with McCaslin."

Casey turned to face the woman.

"What did you say?"

"I said McCaslin sat there and played poker with Wingate most of the day and growled because he couldn't find Buck to do something for him. Rogers said they were kinda tense with each other all day."

Casey felt the trembling begin in her knees and she knew she had to get away. It wasn't Red, either, she thought. Nobody was out there protecting me!

"Miz Lee in here?"

Casey looked toward the door and recognized the Jones boy.

"Yes, I'm over here," she said.

"They's some ladies at your place wants to see you."

Casey pointed to the candy jar on the counter.

"Will you give him one of those, Mrs. Rogers? Just put it on my bill."

As she left the store, Casey looked toward the small cluster of women gathered before her barn.

"What could they want?" she asked herself. "I hope Mrs. Grimley hasn't sent them to haul me off to church tomorrow, or something."

She smiled as she approached the women.

"Good morning. Can I help you?"

One of the women stepped forward.

"Is it true? About the wire, I mean. You have a special price for them that wants it for a garden?"

"Yes, it's true, on any amount up to five rolls. The price is a dollar and a half per roll or one dollar cash and another dollar's worth of plunder."

"Ethel Johnson said you trusted her for some oats."

Casey's mind whirled as she tried to keep pace with this turn of events.

"Do you all need wire?" she asked.

Casey smiled as the heads nodded.

A small woman detached herself from the group.

"I didn't bring no plunder. I didn't know about it till I got to town. Would you trust me?"

They all talked at once and Casey tried to follow the snatches of conversation.

"Me, neither. I traded my stuff to Mrs. Rogers. Them animals. They'll eat it all if they can. It's the deer that drives me crazy."

Casey held up her hand.

"Ladies, I would be glad to have your business and I wouldn't think of letting you leave town without your wire. If you will all step inside, I'll take your orders one at a time; then you can come by and pick up your wire as you leave town."

Casey led the way into her quarters and seated the ones she could in chairs and let the others find themselves a place on the bed. She put the paper on the table before her and picked up the pen.

"I'll write down the names here and the amount of cash you paid. Then I will write out to the side of that, 'Trade.' When you come back to town, you can just bring in whatever you feel is of proper value. Is that fair?"

Casey waited and looked from one to another while each nodded. The small woman stepped up to the table. She hesitated for a moment before she spoke, as though trying to make a decision. Then she opened her reticule and took out a handful of coins and placed them on the table before Casey.

"I'm Jane Smathers and there's two dollars there."

Casey wrote "Jane Smathers" on the paper and started to write "2 rolls." When the woman made a sound, Casey glanced up at her and watched the weatherbeaten face slowly turn crimson.

"I have got to have five rolls of that wire. I'll bring three more dollars and my Texas Star quilt next Saturday."

Casey heard the sudden intake of breath in the room. That quilt must be something, she thought. She scratched out the numeral 2 that she had written, wrote 5 beside it, and listened in amazement to her own words.

"Will you want two-point or four-point wire?"

"What's the difference?"

"Well, there's quite a bit of argument about that," Casey said. "I really think all that is needed is two-point wire. It will hold any kind of stock and there is a little more length to the pound."

"Two-point will be fine," the woman said.

Casey listened to herself again.

"Except for hogs. If you have a hog problem, sometimes it is best to put four-point wire close together near the bottom of the fence. Although the two-point wire will definitely hold hogs if it is put up correctly."

Casey wrote "two-point" beside the Smathers order and listened to the whispers in the room.

"Real businesslike. Expert! Trusts us."

Casey took the orders one by one and collected the cash as the women counted out their money on the table. Each smoothed the crumpled bills a little as they placed the money before Casey.

"It's so hard for them to part with cash," Casey told herself. "I feel sorry for them."

When the orders had been taken, Casey glanced at her stove.

"I have hot water. Would you like some tea, anyone?"

No one spoke but Casey could see some nods. She went to the cabinet, took out cups and the teapot, made the tea, and served everyone.

Casey drank her tea and said as little as possible as the women talked of babies, gardens, and cures for ailments. She listened while they exchanged all the news that they knew.

This is how Mrs. Rogers learns everything, Casey thought. She doesn't even have to ask. She just listens.

The women finished their tea and rose. One by one they said their goodbyes. Casey thanked each of them for her business and listened again to her own words.

"Please come by for tea any time you are in town. My kettle is always on and I would love to have you any time."

"Good Lord! I didn't even know I was going to say that!" she told herself when the last guest left.

Casey put the cash away and unbuckled her gun belt.

Well, that wire has got to be moved out to the front and it's not going to move itself, she thought. It's a lot of work but I did a little business.

Casey started for the door.

"I wonder if Buck would lend me his wheelbarrow," she muttered.

"Just suck now, Harley! It ain't fair to bite!"

Casey went through the door and looked for the owner of the voice. She looked to the right at the Jones boy sitting on her bench. Beside him sat a smaller copy of himself.

The older boy held a peppermint stick, now sucked to a fine needle point. He held it toward the open mouth of the smaller boy.

"Just suck now, Harley, no biting."

Casey watched fascinated as the boy carefully wrapped his lips around the candy and waited while his brother slowly withdrew the pointed stick, then repeated the process for himself.

When they noticed Casey, both boys rose from the bench, held themselves erect, and faced her.

"Ma said we should come thank you for the candy."
Casey laughed.

"That's fine. I'm glad you like it. How would you like to earn money to buy some more?"

"I'd like that mighty well, Miz Lee. I'd like for Harley here to have his own."

Casey sent the boys to Buck's for the wheelbarrow and supervised them as they moved the wire from inside the barn to separate stacks out front.

When the wire had been stacked, she gave each of the boys a nickel and watched them race for Rogers's store.

Casey collapsed on the bench.

"I've had quite a morning," she told herself. "Those women! They loved the wire. Maybe, just maybe, before too long . . ."

Maude's whinney interrupted and Casey raised her head to listen. She doesn't do much of that, she thought. I wonder what can be wrong with her?

Casey rose, walked into the barn, and went to the animal's stall.

"Steady, girl, steady."

Casey kept herself away from Maude. She stood in the aisle behind her and carefully looked to see if there was a snake or small animal causing Maude's restlessness. When she saw nothing, she spoke sternly to Maude.

"Maude, you settle down! Quit stepping around that way! Steady now!"

Casey felt the presence first; then she heard the measured plop, plop of hoofs as Jud Wingate rode the big red stallion through the front door of her barn.

"Oh, God! I can't face him now. Not this soon. What will I do?" she muttered.

Wingate rode the length of the barn, stopped before Casey, and leaned forward in the saddle.

"Casey, who is this Red McCaslin and what is he to you?"

"I think you have met Mr. McCaslin on more than one occasion," Casey snapped.

She smiled a little at Jud's puzzled look.

"I can only think of once. I played poker with him yesterday."

"And just what brought it to your mind that he might be something to me? Did the two of you sit in that saloon and bandy my name about all day?"

"No, your name wasn't mentioned. Once, though, he said for no apparent reason that anyone who wanted to stay alive in this town better not bother the barbed-wire lady."

Jud sat upright in his saddle.

"Casey, I have to know what he is to you!"

Casey stared at the man and then did her best to suppress a giggle and to let her eyes wrinkle at the corners.

"He's a man that does some things a helluva lot better than you do," she said, and jumped back as the red stallion reared at the sudden jerk of the bit.

CHAPTER 29

CASEY sat at her window and watched and hoped for more customers for her wire.

"I've got to sell some more," she told herself. "There's Mother to help and then I've ordered all that wire from Mr. Glidden."

When no customers appeared, she paced the floor and worried.

If Mr. Glidden will get those circulars to me, that may help. She smiled. I just know each one of those women will ask her husband which is better, two-point or four-point wire. And those women have got to be talking to other women. I know the wire will do the job. It held the Stanton bull . . .

Casey looked out the window again and gasped.

"He's got those boys by the ear! He shouldn't do that!"

She waited until he came closer; then she went outside and faced the man. I've never seen anyone so angry, she thought.

"Mr. Jones, can I help you?"

The oldest boy squinted his eye and moved his head the best he could to ease the pain in his ear.

"Ask her, Pa. Ask her quick!"

Casey looked at each of the boys, then at their father.

"Mr. Jones, they are your boys but . . ."

"Did you give these boys a nickel?"

Casey stamped her foot.

"I *paid* them a nickel each. They worked hard moving wire for me and I paid them for it."

Jones released his grip.

I don't know which of the four of us is the most relieved, Casey thought.

"Thank you, ma'am. I am much relieved and much obliged to you. I was, well, I was afraid they had stole the money."

Casey shook her head.

"No, Mr. Jones. They are good honest boys and they worked hard for me."

I hope he lets the matter drop now and doesn't lecture them all the way home, she thought.

Jones nodded to Casey, turned, put his hands on his boys' shoulders, and began to walk away. Then he stopped. The boys beside him stopped too, waiting. After a moment Jones turned to face her, and the boys turned with him.

"Mrs. Lee, could we talk some business?"

"Of course, Mr. Jones."

Casey felt her heart begin to pound.

"Oh, God, I hope he wants to buy some wire," she said to herself.

Casey moved to her bench.

"Have a seat, Mr. Jones, and tell me what kind of business we can do."

The man crouched on the ground facing her.

"Well, Mrs. Lee, you know my place is small and I work out some. I'm helping Grimley now with his fence."

"You got the work, then?"

Jones picked up a stick and scratched in the dirt.

"Yes, ma'am, I'm helping over there, and the more I work with the wire, the better I like it. It's just too practical to do without."

Casey watched him scratch in the dirt again.

I wonder why they do it, she thought. William said it was a sure sign a Texan was thinking if he scratched in the dirt with a stick. The man's voice interrupted.

"Well, I was thinking. I sure need to fence my little place."

"He wants it! He wants some wire!" she told herself.

"Well, Mr. Jones, I'm sure we can handle that," she said.

"Well, ma'am, cash is mighty short."

"Oh, hell!" Casey whispered.

"Ma'am?"

"Nothing. You were saying?"

"As I was saying, cash is mighty short. I heard some of the women talking, and I thought, well, I wondered if maybe I could work for you and work out the price of some of the wire."

Oh, Lord, this whole thing is going to get out of hand. I should never have started trading with those women, Casey thought. She turned her attention back to the man.

"I don't know, Mr. Jones. I really don't have any work for you to do."

When the man rose from his squatting position and turned away, she suddenly felt the cold formality she had seen in other Texas men.

"Sorry to have bothered you, ma'am."

"Now I've offended him," she told herself.

"Mr. Jones, I'm sorry . . ."

Casey held her breath as the man turned back to her and she could tell it was a real effort to pursue the matter further.

"You understand I'm not asking for credit. I'd work it out. I just wanted the same deal you gave the women. I'd pay half cash and work out the other half."

Casey rose from the bench and put her hand on the man's arm.

"Oh, Mr. Jones, I did misunderstand you. You see, I do have to have at least half in cash to pay my supplier. I thought you wanted to work out the full price of the wire and I just can't afford that."

"No, ma'am. I just wanted the same deal you give the women."

Casey sighed and let relief flow through her. I'm glad we got that untangled, she thought. He's a nice man and I don't want to offend him.

"Come inside, Mr. Jones, and we can write up an agreement. You can take your wire whenever you want it." She hesitated. "I don't know yet just what kind of work I'll ask you to do for me."

Casey sat at the table, wrote the agreement, turned it around, pushed it toward Jones, and handed him the pen. She waited while the man held the pen for a moment, then carefully drew an X at the bottom of the page and pushed the paper back to her.

Casey held the paper and scanned what she had written, then she spoke softly.

"Would you like for me to read it to you, Mr. Jones?"

The man rose and stood before her with his hat in his hand.

"No, ma'am. I'll take your word for it. I know what we agreed to and you know. That's enough for me. I only signed the paper because you wanted me to. I'll be back for the wire when I have finished at Grimley's."

Casey nodded, rose, and extended her hand. When he didn't respond, she dropped the hand; then he extended his. They both laughed when finally their hands met.

He's a good man, Casey thought. I can tell he works hard by the feel of his hand. She crossed the room and showed Jones out.

"Thanks for the business, Mr. Jones."

"Thanks for the work, ma'am."

Casey waited for him to walk away but the man stood in place and dug at the door frame with a fingernail.

"Was there something else, Mr. Jones?"

He pried a splinter from the board and looked down at it as he spoke.

"I was thinking. Everyone says you will be fencing your place out there. I thought maybe I could do that for you."

When he looked up at her, Casey could see the excitement in the man's face.

"We could make a real showplace out there," he said. Casey nodded.

"We could," she said. "We sure could."

Jones turned and walked away. Casey closed the door behind him and threw herself on the bed.

"I'm completely worn out," she said aloud. "But I've had a good day."

She closed her eyes and let herself begin to drift into sleep; then she sat upright on the bed. I can't go to sleep now, she thought. Those women will be coming for their wire soon. She sat on the side of the bed and massaged her temples.

"Yes, sir, quite a day," she murmured.

The knock on the door sounded angry somehow and Casey wished she didn't have to answer it. She swung the door open and faced Mrs. Smathers. The woman glared at Casey, then glanced over her shoulder at the man seated on the wagon.

"My man says I can't have no wire. He don't believe in it. He says for me to get my money back!"

Casey tried to conceal her surprise and disappointment.

"Come in, Mrs. Smathers. I'll get your money."

Inside, the woman winked at Casey and spoke in a low voice.

"Don't you pay this no mind," she said. "I'll be back next Saturday and get my wire. I'll have all the money for half and I'm bringing you my Texas Star quilt."

"Whatever you say, Mrs. Smathers," she nodded to indicate the man outside. "Won't he . . . ?"

"He'll be all right by then. He ain't gettin' nothing from me next week but a hard time and grits for every meal. There ain't going to be no beauty in his life whatsoever until he begins to believe in wire."

The woman winked again and Casey handed her the money.

The other women came one by one with their husbands and picked up their wire.

"They looked proud and pleased to be the first to have

the wire," Casey told herself. "I hope the fever spreads."

She waved goodbye to the last customer and turned to go inside. She stopped at the stack of Smathers's wire.

"I'd better take this inside," she muttered and bent to pick up the heavy roll. The weight tugged at her arms; then she felt the prick of a barb.

"To hell with it," she said, and dropped the wire and went inside. She put food on the table and began to eat. She picked up a biscuit and waited for a nudge on her leg.

"I sure miss old Stranger," she murmured.

As she ate, her mind turned to her agreement with Jones.

I could fence my little farm and people passing by would see it and it probably would help sell the wire. Excitement began to fill her at the next thought.

These people are all short of cash, but if I had the place fenced, I could trade for livestock. Horses, maybe. I could keep some of them here for sale. If I can just take in enough cash to cover my cost, I can take my profit in other things and I can keep things going. I know I can!

Casey saw Mrs. Rogers's form pass the window and she had the door open before the woman could knock.

"Come in, lady. Here, let me light a lamp."

Casey lit the lamp while the woman sank into a chair and sighed.

"What a day!" she said.

"You were busy at the store today, I take it," Casey said.

"Yep, it's always that way on Saturday. I'm used to it but Rogers didn't help hardly at all today. Heard you did some business over here, Casey."

"I suppose so. I got some cash and the promise of some plunder next week. I'm not real sure of what I can do with a Texas Star quilt."

Casey watched as Mrs. Rogers jerked herself erect in her chair.

"Did that Smathers woman trade you for her Texas Star quilt?"

Casey nodded.

"Damn her! I've been after that quilt for a year and she would never let me have it. You can sell it to me, that's what you can do with it."

Casey smiled.

"It's yours. I'll bring it to you as soon as I get it. You can just credit my bill for whatever it's worth."

"You don't owe me for anything except one stick of candy."

"I'll bring the quilt anyway if you want it. I'll use it to pay ahead on my bill."

Mrs. Rogers sat back in the chair.

"You've made a deal, Casey," she said.

Casey went to the stove and poured two cups of coffee, served the woman, and then seated herself again. The women sipped their coffee and looked at each other. Then Mrs. Rogers spoke, "I'm worried, Casey."

"What about, Mrs. Rogers?"

"It's those two men of yours."

"Mine? They're not mine."

Mrs. Rogers frowned.

"They are and you know it. You need to marry one of them."

"I have no intention of doing that. Why are you worrying about them? They are both grown men."

Casey watched the frown on Mrs. Rogers's face deepen.

"Stiff-legged."

"What?"

"They're walking around stiff-legged."

Casey put her empty cup in its saucer.

"Whatever do you mean, Mrs. Rogers?"

"Oh, Casey, you've seen two strange dogs come up to one another and walk around and around each other stiff-legged until they get it all settled."

"Yes, I think I have."

"That's the way these two are acting. Been at it all day. They're both too dangerous to be going on that way. If this keeps up, there's going to be a killing, for sure."

Casey put her head in her hands.

"Oh, Lord, Mrs. Rogers, I hope not."

Mrs. Rogers rose and Casey followed her to the door. The sound of Buck's anvil rang in the night.

"Buck's sure staying at it late tonight," Mrs. Rogers said. Then she turned back to Casey.

"Better think about it, Casey. Better marry one of them before you lose them both."

Casey struggled to find some kind of answer for the woman when her thoughts were swept away by the sound of shots.

Mrs. Rogers looked down the street. Casey felt her strength drain away and she clung to the door frame as Mrs. Rogers turned to her with an accusing look.

"Coming, Casey?"

Casey shook her head.

"I can't. Come back and tell me," she gasped. "Please come back and let me know . . ."

Casey clung to the door frame and watched Mrs. Rogers hurry down the street.

CHAPTER 30

CASEY threw herself on her bed, buried her face in the pillow, and wept.

"What have I done? What have I done?" she sobbed again and again. She turned on her back and stared at the ceiling. She clenched her fists until her nails cut into her hands. Then she knelt beside the bed and offered a silent prayer.

"Dear God, let them be all right. Don't let this happen. I can't stand it, God. I can't stand to lose another man . . ."

Stunned at her own prayer, Casey opened her eyes; then she closed them again.

"God," she whispered. "I don't even know which one I'm praying for."

She knelt beside the bed, put her face against the coolness of the sheet, and let tears roll from her eyes.

"I did it. I did it myself. I drove them to it with my smart remarks," she told herself.

She clamped her teeth together and shook till her jaws ached; then she threw herself on the bed, overcome by remorse.

When the door crashed open, Casey jerked herself erect. She turned on the bed and faced Mrs. Rogers as the woman collapsed, gasping, on a chair.

"Who? Tell me who," Casey screamed.

Casey clenched her fists while the woman panted and gasped for air.

"Came. Came as quick as I could."

"Mrs. Rogers, tell me who!"

"McCaslin," the woman gasped.

Casey felt the pain clutch at her heart and she was sure it had torn in two.

"Is he? Is he dead?"

She waited while the woman gasped and shook her head. Then Casey could stand it no longer.

"For God's sake, Rogers! Say something!"

The older woman held her hand to her breast.

"McCaslin shot Anthony."

"Kill him?"

Casey clenched her fists and gritted her teeth while the woman shook her head.

"No. Anthony was drunk and got to shooting his mouth off at McCaslin. He finally worked up the nerve to throw down on Red. Red shot him in the shoulder. Everybody that saw it said it was a fair fight."

"Men!" Casey stormed. "Men and their big pride and their big guns. When I think about myself down there on my knees praying for . . . They just have to shoot each other, don't they? They just won't have it any other way, will they? I cannot understand . . ."

"Casey!"

Casey looked at the woman.

"Casey, you know as well as anybody that sometimes it has to be done."

Mrs. Rogers stared at Casey's shotgun.

Casey looked at her feet.

"I'm not proud of it, Mrs. Rogers," she said. Then she raised her eyes and looked directly at the older woman.

"But I'd do the same thing again," she said.

Mrs. Rogers rose.

"I've got to go. Wanted to let you know what the excitement was about."

"Thank you, Mrs. Rogers. Thank you very much."

As the woman started to walk away, Casey called after her.

"Mrs. Rogers!"

"Yes, Casey."

"Anthony will set Wingate after Red for sure now, won't he?"

Mrs. Rogers was silent for a moment.

"I was hoping you wouldn't think of that tonight," she said and walked into the darkness.

Casey turned away and sat on her bench. She watched the glow of Buck's forge and listened to the ring of his anvil.

"He really is working late tonight," she told herself, and rose to her feet. She sauntered over to the blacksmith shop and stood in the doorway. Buck looked up and smiled.

"Evening, Miz Casey."

"Evening, Buck. You're working late. Hear about the shooting?"

Buck thrust the chunk of iron into the forge.

"Yes, ma'am, I heard." Then he said, "I got a little behind."

Casey moved to the box and seated herself.

"I heard you were closed yesterday, Buck."

Casey lifted a knee, clasped both hands around it, and leaned back.

"I hope you weren't ill."

"Nope."

Casey clasped the knee tighter and rocked back and forth on the box.

"I was closed yesterday, too, Buck."

"Yes'm."

"Yes, Buck, I rode out to Grimley's place."

Buck took the tongs and pushed the iron deeper into the coals.

"Buck, as I rode, someone followed me. He didn't really follow me, just kept pace with me. Stayed with me all day."

Casey watched the man poke at the fire with his tongs and push at the coals until they covered his work.

"Buck, was that you out there, maybe, sort of, looking after me?"

Casey waited while the huge man spat into the fire, then wiped his mouth with his hand.

"Reckon a man can ride wherever he wants, can't he, Miz Casey?"

Casey rose from her box, walked around the forge, and put both hands on his shoulders. When the man leaned toward her, she kissed him on the cheek.

"Thank you, Buck," she said, and walked out the door.

Back in her room, she undressed in the dark and climbed into bed. She lay in the darkness and thought about Buck.

He is such a beautiful man inside. Some woman will be lucky to get him some day. I hope he doesn't do that again, though. He nearly scared me to death. He can't afford the time, either. He has more to do now than he can keep up with.

She closed her eyes and hoped for sleep but sleep would not come. Her mind was a clutter of thoughts.

If I fenced the place . . . The horse business should be good . . . I just hope those women will get the wire going . . . Anyway, we've got a bin full of oats and I'm paid a-head with Mrs. Rogers . . . If I really get the quilt . . . I'll ride out tomorrow and look at the farm and decide about the fencing . . .

Casey turned on her side and pulled her knees up to her stomach.

"I'll ride out there tomorrow," she murmured.

***

Casey woke with a start and stared at the clock on the wall.

"Good Lord! Almost noon!" she said aloud. She scrambled from the bed and hurried into her clothes. She gulped a cold biscuit, strapped on the .38, picked up the shotgun, and carried it into the barn.

She saddled Maude, stuffed the shotgun into the

saddlebag, and led the mare out the front of the barn. Casey stopped and tied the shotgun behind the saddle. She looked toward the blacksmith shop, then down the deserted street. She swung herself into the saddle and walked Maude to Buck's watering trough. She slouched in the saddle while Maude drank.

I'm so tired, she thought.

"Casey! Casey! Casey!"

Casey jerked Maude's head up at the sound of Mrs. Rogers's voice.

"What on earth?" she said. "Here, Mrs. Rogers, over here!"

She watched the woman as she approached, running hard, waving her hands, and screaming at the top of her voice.

"Casey, they're going at it! They're gonna do it! They're coming into the street right now!"

Casey froze and stared at Mrs. Rogers.

"It was Wingate. He called Red out. Sent him word to get out of town."

Casey looked down the street as the pulse pounded in her ears.

That's Jud at the far end, she thought. He's already in the street. That's Red nearest me. I'd know his back anywhere.

Suddenly a feeling of utter desperation overwhelmed her. She drove the spurs hard into Maude's sides.

Casey heard the mare scream with pain as she hunched under the saddle. Casey grabbed for the saddle horn as her head snapped backward. She drove the spurs into the animal again, leaned forward, and shook the reins behind Maude's ears.

Casey closed her eyes and reached for the .38; then she felt Maude's shoulder crash into McCaslin's back. She forced her eyes open in time to see him rolling in the dirt. She snapped her head around and looked over Maude's ears. She saw Jud's fluid movement toward his holster begin;

then she saw him hesitate and, a second later, throw his arms over his face as she rode over him.

She felt the tangle of man and hoofs as Maude stumbled. Casey jerked hard on the reins but couldn't hold the animal.

"My God, we're going down!" she told herself. "I hope I didn't kill them."

She clutched the .38, closed her eyes tight, and tried to roll when she felt the hardness of the ground. When she opened her eyes, she was staring at the sky. She rolled to her stomach, stretched her arms out in front of her, and sighted down the gun barrel.

"I'll shoot if I have to," she told herself.

Over the sight of the .38, she saw McCaslin struggle to his feet. His right arm hung limp and he reached across his body with the left to claw at his holster. Then she saw him fall on his face in the dirt. As his leg crumpled beneath him, Casey scrambled to her feet, ran to Jud, and stopped where he lay in the street.

"Poor darling. I've killed him. I know I've killed him," she told herself.

She knelt in the dirt and kissed the man's face, then rose and ran to McCaslin. Casey felt herself stagger as she ran.

"I've got to know. I've got to know," she said again and again.

She stared straight ahead at Red's form in the street. Darkness moved in closer and closer until she could see the man through only a constantly narrowing circle of light that penetrated the darkness. Then the circle closed completely and she felt her face slam against Red's broad back as she ceased to struggle.

***

Casey sat at the table, read her mail, and, from time to time, spoke to the man in the bed.

"Mr. Glidden writes that the circulars and the new shipment of wire are on the way."

"If you loved me, you wouldn't try to keep me in this bed."

"Mr. Glidden says the wire is beginning to move better all the time. He says it is due to people of vision like me."

"Anybody that would hide a man's crutch . . ."

"And he says that he hopes to be coming out this way before winter."

"I'm going to stand up and hop around until I find that crutch!"

Casey put the letter from Glidden aside, opened the next one, and read it.

"I don't see how you can hide anything as big as a crutch in this one little room."

"It's from Mother. She says she is working in the law office now and Father is better and looking for work."

"I didn't even know your father was out of work. Dammit, where's that crutch?"

Casey opened the next letter and began to read.

"Oh, this one's from Gaylord!"

"Who?"

"Fontaine. Gaylord Fontaine."

"Casey! The crutch please!"

"Listen to this! Oh, my goodness! Well, maybe. Listen to this. I'll read it all to you."

Casey smoothed the letter and began to read.

Dear Mrs. Lee:

I take my pen in hand at long last to write you again.

Casey stopped and looked toward the man on the bed. "Gaylord talks like that, you know," she said, and continued to read.

Mr. Glidden is most pleased with the good start you have made in selling the wire there. I want to thank you for the part you have played in my success with the Glidden Company.

On my most recent trip to the home office, Mr. Glidden introduced me to a man named McCormick and said we should get together. Mr. McCormick and I struck a bargain. Now for the part that I am almost afraid to mention. I have once again made a bold and presumptuous move. I have shipped you, on consignment, three McCormick reapers. All you have to do is sell them for . . .

The loud voice drowned out Casey's reading.

"Casey McCaslin! You get over here or you're going to have me to deal with!"

Casey took the last letter from the table and carried it unopened to the stove. She lifted the cap of the stove and stood for a moment, reading the return address:

> Judson Wingate
> General Delivery
> Waco, Texas

She dropped the sealed envelope on the coals and watched the paper turn brown, then burst into flames.

"Poor darling," she whispered as the flames grew.

"Casey!"

Casey turned, moved to the edge of the bed, and began to disrobe.

"Still want the crutch?" she asked.